With surprising strength for one hovering on the brink, his lordship pulled her tight against his chest.

"What are you doing?" she gazed up to demand as he bent his head to kiss her. She was too astonished by this development to think of extracting herself from such a shocking intimacy. Then, after a bit, when the issue of propriety did niggle, it seemed best to humor a man who might well succumb to the Grim Reaper at any moment.

But when he at last released her and she had caught her breath, her sensibilities sorted themselves sufficiently for her to glare at him. His lordship appeared unable to meet her eyes. Shame, she had supposed, till he leaned back against the tree trunk and began to chuckle.

Also by Marian Devon
Published by Fawcett Books:

MISS ARMSTEAD WEARS BLACK GLOVES
MISS ROMNEY FLIES TOO HIGH
M'LADY RIDES FOR A FALL
SCANDAL BROTH
SIR SHAM
A QUESTION OF CLASS
ESCAPADE
FORTUNES OF THE HEART
MISS OSBORNE MISBEHAVES
LADY HARRIET TAKES CHARGE

MISTLETOE AND FOLLY

Marian Devon

FAWCETT CREST • NEW YORK

A Fawcett Crest Book
Published by Ballantine Books
 Published in the United States by Ballantine Books, a division of Random House, Inc., New York, and simultaneously in Canada by Random House of Canada Limited, Toronto.

Library of Congress Catalog Card Number: 91-92195

ISBN 0-449-21739-6

Manufactured in the United States of America

First Edition: December 1991

Chapter One

"THE MATTER IS not open to discussion, Jemima." Mrs. Forbes's scissors snapped a thread for emphasis. Her usually amiable, still pretty countenance grew stern. "You will spend Christmas at Lawford Court."

"But I haven't been invited," her daughter protested as she laid aside the nightgown she'd just mended and pulled a ripped petticoat from the work-basket. It was a last-ditch argument, and a futile one at that, but it was not in her nature to accept a situation meekly that she found intolerable in the extreme.

"Perhaps not in the particular," her mother conceded, respecting her daughter's face-saving pursuit of a lost cause. "Your aunt did mention Clarissa specifically. But she also declared she felt a duty toward her widowed sister's family. And high time, too, I must say." The scissors clicked again, viciously this time, and Jemima gave her mother a startled look.

It was uncharacteristic for this almost saintly lady to be out of charity with anyone. She had borne up well when five births had failed to produce a male heir. Then, when her husband had died and the entailed estate had gone to a distant cousin, she had uncomplainingly removed her young brood to a small cottage. Some sacrifices she had not been prepared to make, however. The walls of the withdrawing room, where she and her second eldest were now working, fairly bulged with an excess of furniture she'd refused to leave behind at their former manor house.

Aware of her daughter's shocked reaction, Mrs. Forbes forced an apologetic smile. "I should not have spoken sharply. My sister, I'm sure, has not intended neglect. Like most of us, she has simply been taken up with her own affairs."

"With the affairs of that loose-fish, Marcus, more likely."

"That's no way to speak of your cousin, Jemima. The point I was attempting to make is that even though my sister mentioned Clarissa specifically in her invitation, she of course had no way of knowing that your sister is indisposed."

"Indisposed!" Jemima chuckled. "That's certainly a delicate way of stating the case."

Her mother looked pained. "Really, it's quite beyond me why you seem to find your sister's malady humorous. I should think you might instead be sympathetic."

"Well, you must admit it is a bit ridiculous to come down with a case of measles at age twenty. Most folk are still in the nursery when they have them. And how Clarissa managed to escape when the rest of us had measles and then succumbed with little Edith is past all understanding.

"But I am sympathetic, Mama. Truly. I've read to her until I'm hoarse. Every word, at least twice, of that prosy periodical she likes so much. Really, that editor hadn't the slightest notion of the torture he was causing all her kith and kin when he chose to publish Clarissa's poem in his rag."

"I must own I wasn't best pleased by it," her mother sighed. "It somehow seems—unladylike—to write for money."

"Well, when it comes to that, the payment was far too small to rate as commerce. And since Clarissa's name didn't appear, no harm was done."

That sanguine observation was received in silence, neither lady being quite sure of the level of harm that might have been incurred.

"Well, I will admit," Mrs. Forbes picked up the reins of their former topic, "that I wish it were Clarissa who was going to the Court for Christmas. She's far too inclined to dream her life away and needs to go more into society."

"Needs to meet eligible young men, you mean."

"Yes, I do mean that," her mother replied evenly. "With five daughters to settle and less than a competency to go on with, I'm in no position to let any opportunity pass that could work to my daughters' advantage. And that is why I'm determined to make the most of my sister's invitation. If not with Clarissa, then with you."

"But you know that Aunt Lawford and I do not deal well together. And as for that toad Marcus—"

"Jemima, that will do! You were only thirteen when we last visited Lawford Court. I can only hope that in these six years you've overcome your youthful tendency for hoydenism."

"But the point is, Mama, our aunt was quite taken with Clarissa at the time, and it's no good thinking she'll be pleased by my substitution."

"She'll have no cause to be displeased if you curb your tongue and mind your manners. Which is certainly what I expect of you," Mrs. Forbes said sternly.

"Yes, but what of the young man she's asked for Clarissa? It hardly stands to reason that he and I would suit. Think of the poor gentleman's disappointment."

"Now you're being absurd, Jemima. You are every bit as attractive as your older sister. Who, I don't mind saying is very pretty indeed. And, thank goodness, dark hair and eyes are quite the fashion now, or so I'm told. No gentleman is going to be disappointed in your . . . appearance."

"Well if he's been led to expect sweet, soft-spoken Clarissa, he will be. And though I promise to try to behave . . . well, you know what they say about leopards and spots, which doesn't make much sense because leopards don't have any, but you know what I mean. I can't become another creature entirely."

"I realize that, dear." And though Mrs. Forbes did not actually utter the words "more's the pity," they did rather seem to hover in the air. "But as for the young man who has been invited for poor Clarissa, I can't imagine that your aunt has put any real thought into making a suitable matchup. But even supposing that she has done so and the two of you do not deal well together, that shouldn't really matter. For according to Ada, Sir Walter is quite determined to celebrate Christmas in the old manner and fill his house from top to bottom with relatives and friends. So you are almost certain to find some congenial young folk among the company."

"Cousin Marcus's friends? You must be funning. Still, perhaps you're right. There may be other poor relations like myself there and we can all huddle together below the salt."

"Jemima, that will do!" Mrs. Forbes's frown was terrible, and her daughter realized that she'd gone too far. "I shall have you know that in all save fortune your father's family is the superior of the Lawfords, and I shall expect you to conduct yourself accordingly. But we're wasting time in this pointless discussion when we need to decide upon your wardrobe. I will not have you appearing shabby. Thank goodness you and Clarissa are of a size. You will, of course, take her new sprigged muslin. And her traveling cloak."

While Mrs. Forbes strived to creatively combine her daughters's wardrobes, Jemima's mind strayed to other matters.

"Will my aunt be sending a carriage for me?" she inquired.

"No," her mother reluctantly admitted. "You're to go by public coach."

I might have known, the old pinch-penny! But Jemima was learning. She kept the observation to herself.

Chapter Two

Miss Jemima Forbes was feeling not at all the thing. In point of fact, she was decidedly queasy. Riding backward had never agreed with her, and the erratic progress of the coach, coupled with its miserable springs, was threatening to undo her. She wondered what would happen if she reached across the farmer's wife beside her and lowered the window. Fresh air would be a welcome thing to dilute the mixture of odors emanating from a basket on that matron's lap. There was mincemeat, most likely; an overripe cheese for certain. But worst of all, the woman had proudly mentioned a dressed goose that had surely grown suspect.

Jemima looked at the window longingly. The rain that had pelted the coach at the beginning of their journey had abated, but the drops it had left behind were now frozen on the glass. She abandoned the notion of lowering it. She would undoubtedly be murdered by the other passengers crammed together in the Dover Mail.

The coach hit a pothole and sent them bouncing amid gasps and shrieks and one shocking oath. "That confounded coachman ain't missed a single rut in the road since Canterbury," the source of the blasphemy, a young tar on the way to rejoin his ship, declared.

"Are you all right, Bess?" Jemima looked at her maid anxiously. The chubby young woman had taken on a decidedly greenish cast. She merely groaned in reply. Jemima did hope Bess was suffering nothing more than motion sickness, but she feared the worst.

She had protested against bringing the servant along. "You need Bess here, Mama. Besides, I can do my own hair better than she does." She had gone on to point out that since the coach passed directly by the entrance to her uncle's estate, and since the coachman would be tipped to set her down there, there was really no need for chaperonage. But her mother had been adamant. No daughter of hers would travel alone. It was bad enough to be reduced to public transportation without being shockingly improper as well. Jemima had ceased to argue, aware at last of the overriding reason: her Mama did not wish to lose caste before her wealthy sister.

"It shouldn't be much farther now." Jemima reached across to pat her maid's plump knee. She had persuaded the farmer's wife to exchange seats with Bess a few miles back. The swap had the double benefit of allowing Bess a forward motion and getting the noxious basket out from underneath her nose. The country woman had opened her mouth to object, but one look at Bess's face had changed her mind. All that was needed on this miserable morning was for someone to cast up his or her accounts.

Jemima gazed past the farmer's wife at the road that they'd just traveled and tried to think bright thoughts. This was no easy task; resentment was building. What would it have cost her nabob aunt to have sent a carriage to Chatham to fetch them? Or for that matter, a pony cart. Anything that didn't require being jammed together like pickles in a jar with a scruffy group of holiday travelers. She didn't ask for much. Certainly not for a bang-up rig like the one rapidly overtaking them.

Too rapidly by half!

"Oh my heavens!" Jemima shrieked as a blur of gray horse flesh, a streak of bright red harness, a glimpse of a multicaped gray greatcoat, and a flash of rich red leather and gleaming ebony wood whizzed by them, a mere hairsbreadth from the basket woman's window. Their coach lurched sickeningly, the whinnying of its four horses rivaling the cries of the interior and exterior passengers as it headed for the ditch.

It seemed miraculous that after they had been untangled and extracted no one inside the coach was hurt. It was even more miraculous that the passengers on top, comprised entirely of schoolboys on their way home for Christmas holiday, had been agile and alert enough to jump clear as the coach rolled over and, save for a sprained ankle here and there, were also uninjured.

The coach had not fared as well. An axle had been broken. The sailor volunteered to ride to the next posting house for help and the coachman was unharnessing one of the horses for him when Jemima approached. He was castigating the "damned toffs who think they own the roads" with a string of oaths when she cut through the flow with some assiduous throat clearing.

"Beg pardon, I'm sure, miss." The driver turned toward her, and she tried not to flinch before the redirected powerful fumes of brandy. The cutting wind, still damp with recent rain, was not entirely to blame for his florid cheeks and nose, she concluded. His broad face with its excessive chins was meant to exude the same cheerfulness as the huge holly buttonhole he wore. But now it bestowed a martyred look upon her as if to say, What next?

He answered her inquiries politely, however, assuring her that the entrance to Lawford Court was indeed within walking distance, and, yes, certainly when the repairs had been completed he'd set both her maid and her baggage down there.

Bess insisted that she was going, too, that it would be as good as her life if Mrs. Forbes were to find she'd let her young mistress set out alone. But when she tried to rise from the box Jemima had placed for her on the roadside, she all but fainted.

"Don't be ridiculous," her mistress scolded. "Why I'd have to end up carrying you. Nothing's going to happen to me. Stop holding my cloak, for goodness sake, and I'll have someone back here to fetch you in no time."

That proved to be an optimistic prediction. As Jemima trudged down the highway, Clarissa's cloak was turned into a sail by the strong wind. She clutched it about her as best she could while her cold, wet feet cried out for pattens. She could only conclude that what the coachman considered an "easy walk" when perched behind four mettlesome horses was a far cry from the step-by-step reality.

She was toying with the notion of resting on a large rock that she spied just up ahead when the sound of wheels and horse hooves diverted her. She raised her head, lowered against the wind, to see a cart approaching. Sighing, she abandoned the well-worn track for the muddy verge. The cart had almost passed her by when the driver, obviously startled to see a well-dressed young lady trudging through the countryside alone, clucked his plodding cob to a standstill. "Oh, I say there, miss." He politely raised a battered beaver, but quickly clapped it down again as an icy blast ruffled his light brown hair. "Are you quite all right?"

If her appearance had startled the driver of the cart, Jemima was equally amazed at his. She had fully expected some farmer on his way, possibly, to inspect a field. But the man's voice clearly bespoke the gentleman, as did his well-tailored, though, on second glance, decidedly threadbare, greatcoat.

She explained her predicament, and the gentleman expressed his sympathy. He had a pleasant face, handsome though rather heavily lined for someone Jemima judged to be not quite middle-aged. His gray eyes were a trifle blood-shot, but that condition failed to mask their genuine concern.

"Lawford Court's still a good two miles away," he informed her. "You look absolutely fagged. Here, allow me to take you."

She was explaining that the Court lay in the direction he'd just come from and that she really didn't mind the walk, while at the same time imagining what her mother would have to say to her accepting a ride from a total stranger when her protests were cut short by the sound of racing horses.

"Move it, Dobbin!" The cart owner slapped the cob's rump sharply with the reins and the animal vacated the center of the highway, barely in the nick of time. Two grays pulling a shiny black curricle with red upholstery were speeding toward them.

Once more the near miss came as a streaky blur.

The curricle thundered by, straight through a puddle that erupted in an arc of muddy water. "Blast you!" Miss Forbes screamed, but her words were no doubt lost in the pounding of eight hooves. At any rate the driver neither slowed not turned to look.

"Of all the arrogant, unspeakable, insufferable—!" she fumed, then looked down at Clarissa's mud-splattered traveling cloak and groaned.

The shabby gentleman, who had turned his cart to join her, clucked sympathetically. "Oh, I wouldn't do that if I were you," he advised as she began to dab at the mess with her handkerchief. "Best let it dry first, and then it should brush off all right. At least that's what my ex-valet used to say."

"This really is the last and final straw!" Jemima gingerly folded her muddy handkerchief clean side out and returned it to her reticule. "That bedlamite should be locked up for everyone's protection. I'll have you know that he's the one who ran the Dover Mail right off the road."

"Indeed?" The shabby gentleman had jumped down and was helping Jemima into his cart. (The question of whether or not she should accept his offer had died aborning.) "That's rather strange. Considering his remarkable speed, you'd think by now he'd be at least halfway to Dover. Of course, he could have stopped to rest his cattle. God knows they'd soon need a breather." The man clucked at his cob who plodded off at a stodgy pace, made to seem more plodding in contrast to the magnificent bits of blood that had almost overrun them.

"That is odd," Jemima agreed. "For I certainly didn't pass them. I'd have given him the tongue-lashing of his life if I had done." She mulled the matter over and came up with a solution. "He must have stopped to see someone. I recall passing a gate a few miles back."

"That would have been mine," her companion said, "and I'm afraid I don't number anyone so bang-up-to-the-nines among my acquaintances. By the by, in all the excitement I haven't introduced myself. I'm Edward Baldwin. And my estate, at least what's left of it," he grimaced, "marches next to your uncle's."

Jemima acknowledged his introduction rather absently. Her mind was still on the flashy curricle. "I don't see how I could have mistaken the matter. Granted, in both instances there was very little time for observation, but the rig is quite distinctive. And I could have sworn that the driver who caused our wreck wore that same gray greatcoat. And there could not be two such sap-skulls abroad, surely."

He laughed. "Well actually there could be, you know. Perhaps he . . . they . . . are members of some driving club required to have identical equipages and styles of dress. Like the Four-in-Hand Club, for instance. There's most likely some wager afoot."

"Well, perhaps you're right. I did have a vague impression there were two men in the first carriage. Well, we'll never know," Jemima said regretfully as she put aside several diabolical schemes for her revenge.

"At least we won't unless there's a third one coming," the other said, then chuckled as Jemima looked apprehensively over her shoulder.

Mr. Baldwin proved to be a charming companion. And he managed to find out a great deal about her without revealing much about himself, she later recalled. The highway skirted for a considerable distance along the stone wall of an immense park. She was almost sorry when they came to an entrance and he clucked his cob to a standstill in front of an imposing iron gate whose stark utilitarian bars were surmounted by a fanciful riot of ornate scrolls and flowers.

"I'm afraid you still have quite a distance to walk once you're inside," he said apologetically. "I'm sorry that I can't take you right to the door. But the fact is," he smiled a twisted smile, "I'm by way of being *persona non grata* at the court these days, and it wouldn't do for you to be seen arriving with me." He handed her down from the rickety cart with all the aplomb associated with a crested carriage. Jemima found herself responding to his charming smile with a profusion of thanks that, under the circumstances, might have seemed excessive.

"I do hope that the remainder of your visit will eclipse its bad beginning," he said earnestly, "and I'm sure it will. Sir Walter is noted for his hospitality at any time and particularly during this festive season. Now if you'll just give the bell a pull I'm sure a porter will be Johnny-on-the-spot. Happy Christmas to you, Miss Forbes."

And with a tip of his battered beaver, Mr. Baldwin climbed back into his cart and clucked at his nag. He did not seem to feel it appropriate to wait to see if Jemima was indeed admitted into Lawford Park.

Chapter Three

THE BELL CLANGED loudly. And in the distance she heard hounds baying in response. The echoes had not died away before an ancient lady in an old-fashioned neckerchief and stomacher popped out of the gatehouse almost hidden by trees and shrubbery. As she swung back the well-oiled gates she seemed to think it necessary to apologize for the absence of her son. To make up for this slight she pointed out a path through a wood that provided a shorter route to Lawford Court than the winding carriage road.

Jemima had ample time to observe her uncle's house as she emerged from the wooded area with still a good half mile to go. It was a building of considerable magnitude and much variety, reflecting several centuries of architectural caprice. One wing appeared very old indeed, with heavy stone-shafted bow windows made up of tiny, diamond panes of glass. The majority of the structure reflected a French flavor, which was popular in Charles II's time, while the latest addition smacked of the English Georges.

As she threaded her way through a mazelike formal garden, Jemima's perusal was cut short. She found herself suddenly surrounded by the rowdy pack of dogs whose baying she had heard earlier. Fortunately, they were inclined to be welcoming rather than hostile. But the addition of muddy paw prints to the splatters already on her sister's brand-new cloak was enough to fire her temper, previously cooled by Mr. Baldwin's charm, back on the boil. The disapproving expression on the face of the towering figure who answered her knock did nothing to restore her good humor.

Nor did her aunt's expression as Jemima was ushered into her chamber. Lady Lawford was lying upon a rosewood couch, eyes closed, in a cluttered room that was overpoweringly pink from the cabbage roses upon the silk wall covering to the aubusson carpet and the heavy demask bed and window hangings. The eyes opened, then widened with horror at the sight of her sister's second child. "What on earth!" she exclaimed.

Her ladyship had once been a pretty woman, but that beauty had become obscured by layers of flesh. She strove to make up for this betrayal with a riot of suspiciously golden curls that framed her frilly cap. She pushed herself upright with some difficulty while her eyes traveled from her niece's wind-tangled hair down the length of her spackled cloak to her muddy slippers. "You cannot be Clarissa," she moaned.

"No, Aunt. I'm Jemima. Clarissa took ill and could not come. Since Mama felt you were anxious to entertain *some* member of our family, she sent me instead." This preposterous statement had a predictable effect.

"Well it's hardly the same, now is it? How inconsiderate of Charlotte! To send me a schoolroom miss instead of the young lady whom I specifically invited. It's not as if we don't have enough children in the house already. And now of all times. I can't imagine what Sir Walter was thinking. But never mind. What's done's done. But I must say, Jemima, that it shows a decided want of respect to arrive here looking like some rag-tag gypsy."

"What it shows, Aunt, is that I've been in a coach accident, and, as a consequence, forced to walk for several miles down a muddy highway where I was splattered by some maniac driving a racing curricle. And," she added as some sort of clincher, "I'm nineteen."

If she had expected any kind of sympathetic response, Jemima was doomed to disappointment. "Well, I must say that you still look the hoydenish child whom I remember. I recall telling your mother that she really did not need a son, except for that odious entail, of course, for you were capable of getting into enough mischief for a dozen boys. And I can see that you have not changed."

"I was hardly responsible for my coach breaking an axle, Aunt. But now if—"

"No, I did not suppose you were," Lady Lawford interrupted. "But let me impress upon you, Jemima, the importance of conducting yourself in such a manner as not to reflect poorly upon the family. For I'm certain that you've not the slightest notion of who our guest of honor is." The peevish face grew animated as she waited expectantly for some response.

Jemima bit back the words, *You're right. I'm not a mind reader*. She said instead, "Actually I was given to understand that this was a family gathering."

"Well, it is, for the most part. Which makes it even more wonderful that his lordship would condescend to come. Of course he *is* related. But so distantly that Sir Walter was amazed that he was aware of the kinship. But it just goes to show. Blood is thicker than . . . whatever. For he never goes anywhere but to the most tonish establishments, you see. And not always to those. London's leading hostesses would kill to have him at their parties. For even his most brief appearance is enough to insure that they are all the crack. I can hardly wait," she crowed, "to get back to town and see the expression on that haughty Lady Epworth's face when I tell her who spent Christmas with us at the court."

"Who?"

"Lord Montague!" There was a reverent pause while Lady Lawford looked at her niece expectantly.

"I never heard of him."

Jemima received a stare of withering contempt. "Well, that certainly speaks volumes. Everyone who is anyone has heard of the Viscount Montague. He's simply the most sought-after bachelor in London. He belongs to the most exclusive clubs, is possessed of the largest fortune, has the good looks of an Adonis, and, according to Marcus, is a regular nonesuch when it comes to all the sporting activities that gentlemen seem to value."

"Indeed? And is he the one you invited for Clarissa?"

Lady Lawford's snort was ungenteel but most expressive. "Pray do not be absurd. Lord Montague is so far above Clarissa's touch as to make the notion ludicrous. I wouldn't dream of appearing to promote such an unequal match. And I will not allow you to put yourself forward, Jemima."

She fortunately rushed on before Miss Forbes could utter the retort poised and ready on her tongue. "No, I intend to see to it that his lordship receives the deference that is his due. Both Marcus and I have endeavored to make all of Sir Walter's countrified relations aware of the singular honor of being under the same roof with Lord Montague. You've no idea of how set up my dear boy is over the visit. Marcus has idolized his lordship for donkey's years. As have all the young gentlemen in his set, so I understand. Why Lord Montague has only to tie his neckcloth in a certain fashion for the entire ton to ape it. Marcus has been plaguing his father for weeks now to allow him to purchase a curricle with red leather seats merely because—"

"A *black* curricle with red leather seats?" Jemima interrupted.

"Why, yes. And why Sir Walter has to be so tight-fisted I'll never understand. I should think he would wish to promote—"

"The owner of a black curricle with red leather upholstery is staying *here*?"

"You really must not keep interrupting in that odious fashion, Jemima. I should have hoped my sister had taught you better manners. I have been at some pains to impress upon you that we have a young gentleman of the first stare staying here, and why you should only be impressed by his equipage is quite beyond me. But you mustn't go on standing here. Dinner will be served in just one hour. And it will certainly take you at least that long to become presentable."

Jemima once more pointed out, with what she considered remarkable forbearance, that unless her sick maid and her boxes were fetched from the side of the highway she had no prospect of ever becoming presentable. Lady Lawford, after speaking her mind plainly on the inconvenience of sending a rig to fetch them, agreed to do so. "Though it does seem the outside of enough to be saddled with a sick servant when the household is completely on its ears," she complained. "I can't imagine what possessed my sister."

"Mama had no notion that Bess was ailing, I assure you." Again Jemima demonstrated a remarkable restraint that would have amazed her family, given the fact that she was seething.

"Humph. Well, Riggs," her ladyship nodded to the butler who had remained hovering in the background, "take Miss Forbes to the blue room. I suppose you'll have to come to dinner in your traveling dress, Jemima. Unless you'd prefer to eat in your room?" she offered hopefully, then quickly changed her mind. "No, I'm sure the servants have enough to do without that added burden. Just try to remain inconspicuous."

"And," Jemima muttered as she followed the butler down the hall, "if his High and Mightiness should have the misfortune to clap his eyes on me, I suppose she expects me to bow and scrape and pull my forelock."

For the merest instance the butler's shoulders actually shook as he proceeded toward the tiny cubicle that had been assigned to his employer's niece. This august presence was quite unaware that he had lost his following. Jemima had turned to stone in front of an open door.

A manservant was just emerging from a large bedchamber, carrying a filled basin. Jemima was barely aware of him, however. Her eyes were riveted upon the young gentleman inside.

True, she had only been afforded two glimpses of the man now surveying himself in the looking glass. But his image must have registered somehow in the recesses of her mind. For Jemima was positive that she recognized the profile, especially that arrogant, aristocratic, slightly hawkish nose. The silver-blond hair had, of course, been covered by a beaver. Nor could she have seen the black hard eyes that suddenly cut her way.

Not one to be easily intimidated, especially when her cause was just, Jemima stepped inside the bedchamber and launched an attack.

"Do you, sir, happen to drive a black racing curricle with red leather seats?"

The dark eyes swept her muddied apparel but did not change expression. "I do."

"And just what, sir, makes you think you own the highway?"

"I can assure you that I labor under no such impression." The eyes dismissed her and turned back to the looking glass while he moved one end of his neckcloth an infinitesimal distance and carefully surveyed the effect.

"Don't tell me you were unaware that you forced the public coach off the highway and caused it to capsize into the ditch. I should like to believe so, for it is beyond me, sir, how anyone could be so unfeeling as to cause an accident and then ride on as if nothing at all had happened. Didn't it bother you that someone might have been killed?"

The eyes turned her way again. There were tiny lines and dark circles around them that might indicate he suffered from the headache. Jemima hoped so.

"And was someone killed?" he inquired coldly.

"No," she admitted. "But there were bruises enough— and sprained ankles—and people screaming, scared half out of their wits. My maid, who was ill already, became quite hysterical and has probably caught her death from waiting in the cold."

She paused to catch her breath and glared indignantly. If she had expected the accused to look conscience-stricken, she was doomed to disappointment. If his face reflected anything, it was boredom.

"Have you nothing to say for yourself?" she demanded. "You certainly had no way of knowing that there were no serious injuries. The most heathen wretch imaginable would have turned back to try and rectify the damage he had caused."

This time the gentleman did accord her his full attention. He turned from the glass to level her with a haughty stare. "I did not turn back, Miss Whoever You Are, because, in the first place, it was not convenient to do so, and, in the second, the accident did not appear serious, as you have just admitted."

"I admitted no such thing. It might not have appeared serious to one comfortably perched upon red leather, but I can assure you that to one being rattled around in the interior of the coach like . . . like . . ."

"Ninepins?"

"No indeed! Ninepins do not begin to convey the idea. They simply roll over neatly upon their sides. They don't bounce about till their teeth rattle, then wind up among a pile of screeching humanity."

"Sorry if my metaphor's not up to snuff. But the third reason for not turning back which I was about to offer is that I was in no way responsible for that coach's accident. So I'd advise you to redirect your fishwife tirade where it might do some good—upon your coachman. I had all the room in the world to pass, and if he had not jerked his cattle like a green 'un, he'd not have landed you in your ditch. I collect, however, that besides being cow-handed, he was foxed. Certainly his progress had been erratic from the time I first sighted him. And now if you'll excuse me." He walked over to a four-poster bed and picked up the black long-tailed coat laid out upon it. "I must dress for dinner, and I suggest that you do likewise." He began, with some difficulty, to shrug into his coat. The end result was well worth the effort though. The garment fit him like a well-made glove.

Jemima had been forced to admit to herself, reluctantly, that there might have been a grain of truth in what he'd just said about the coachman's culpability. Even so, this did not excuse the gentleman's callousness and she said as much. "And what's more," she added as her anger reignited, "as if it were not enough that you had caused my coach to wreck and forced me to walk for miles, well then here you came along again and splashed me with muddy water!"

This time she had the satisfaction of seeing the impassive face look fleetingly disconcerted. She pushed home her advantage. "You may be a nonesuch to London society, sir, but to my way of thinking you are just the sort of heedless, spoiled aristocrat that justified the French Revolution."

This struck Jemima as a thoroughly satisfying exit line. She swept from the room without a backward glance, almost running into the returning servant as she did so. Two things struck her simultaneously: one, that the butler had remained well within earshot while she'd been ringing a peal over Lord Montague; and, two, that she'd somehow managed to notice, without consciously registering the fact, that the empty basin the servant now carried underneath his arm had previously been filled with bloody water.

Chapter Four

JEMIMA STOOD BY a window in her cramped bedchamber vigorously brushing at Clarissa's cloak. As Mr. Baldwin had prophesied, it was showing signs of possible redemption when she was interrupted by a pounding on the door. "Come in" was only halfway out of her mouth when that door sprang open and an irate young man stormed inside.

He was wearing evening clothes, as dandified as Beau Brummel's edict of sobriety in fashion would allow. His shirt points were so high as to threaten his ears, his shoulders so wide as to defy physiognomy. His waists was pinched by his satin waistcoat to the point of pain. He gleamed with diamonds at his throat and fob, and his mouse-colored hair had been curled with papers and then swept forward in the Brutus style.

But none of these attempts at elegance was reflected in his face, unprepossessing at best with pale blue eyes that bulged a bit and a chin that receded in compensation. But now the usually pale complexion was suffused with an angry flush, and the eyes threatened to pop right out of his head with indignation. As he crossed the room to stand glaring at Jemima he looked indeed like an adolescent on the verge of a fit and so she judged him. "You . . . you . . .

you . . . how d-dare you! And it's not as t-though you were even invited. Mama s-specifically asked for Clarissa."

"And a good evening to you, too, Marcus." Jemima favored her cousin with a beaming smile purely for the joy of plaguing him further. "It's nice to see that you've actually grown a bit. When I last saw you, when we were . . . what? Thirteen? I vow I thought you were destined to be a midget. Now I do believe you're as tall as I am. Which is quite average. For a woman."

"I'm a good two inches taller than you," he was stung into replying. "And you damned well know it."

"No, really? Well I'll not believe it. Shall we stand back to back before the looking glass?"

"No, we won't, dammit. And I'll thank you to quit trying to change the subject."

"Change the subject? How could I possibly do that? I wasn't even aware we had one."

"Well, we damned well do."

"That, then, is unfortunate, Marcus. For if you don't mind your language, it will die aborning. So say what you have to say without any more profanity."

He looked momentarily abashed but then succumbed once more to his indignation. "It's enough to make a saint swear. I'm dam—dashed if it isn't. How you could just waltz into a cove's house—and, yes, by God—by Gad—*uninvited*—and then rip into the most important guest who's ever graced these halls or is ever likely to like a-a-*harridan* is past all belief. Why it will not surprise me one bit if Montague packs up and leaves this very night." Tears sprang to his eyes. "And h-he'd just given me leave to call him Monty."

"Monty? Well, well, well. Personally I can think of several other names I'd as lief call him."

"You won't call him anything," her cousin screeched. "If he does decide to stay, and you've obviously no idea of just how condescending it was of him to come here in the first place, I'm warning you, from now on stay as far away from Lord Montague as possible."

"Oh, is that why you've come here? Well then I can set your mind at ease. Which I'm anxious to do since I fear that if you swell up any more your waistcoat will cut you quite in two. You see, Marcus, for once in our lives we're in full accord. There's nothing I'd rather do than stay as far away as possible from the odious Lord Montague. And may I suggest that you do the same? It does your consequence no good at all to turn into a sycophantic toadeater."

"Toadeater!"

"That's what I said. How you can fawn over that despicable sprig of the nobility defies me. I should think you'd have more pride."

"Pride! Pride! I'll give you pride!" He was swelling dangerously again. "Have you any idea—no, of course you couldn't have, a nobody from the backwaters like yourself—of just what it means to belong to the Montague set? Why coves will be falling over themselves to wheedle an introduction. I'll be on every hostess's guest list. Why it won't astonish me in the least if I'm asked to join the Four-in-Hand Club. Oh I'll be of the first stare without a doubt. That is unless my horror of a country cousin has so offended—" The sound of a distant thwacking cut off his breath. "Oh, my God!" He looked appalled. "He's doing it! He's actually doing it! I particularly told him not to. Oh God, what will Monty think. W-why can't they ring a bell—or a gong—or better yet, just let Riggs announce the d-damned dinner like any sane household."

"But what on earth is it?" Jemima asked as three hollow thuds again assailed her ears.

"It's Cook. Telling the world that dinner's ready by beating his damned rolling pin on the dresser to call the servants. And Papa put him up to it. Him and his curst Old Christmas. I'd best find Monty and explain." Marcus was running for the door. "I vow he'll think he's arrived in Bedlam."

"Toadeater!" Jemima called after him.

"Vixen!" he yelled back.

"Well at least Cousin Marcus and I are still on normal terms." She grinned to herself as she turned back to the business of Clarissa's cloak.

The rolling pin thwacking had not produced immediate results. So Jemima discovered when she rushed breathlessly into the great hall. Delayed as she'd been by the arrival of Bess and her boxes and the tasks of seeing the former put straight to bed in the servants' quarters and unpacking a gown for herself, she'd fully expected to find the company already at their dinner. But since that clearly was not the case, she could only conclude that the guests had been at a loss to interpret the odd signal.

She looked around the room with considerable curiosity. It was located in the older portion of the house and had clung to its antiquity. The hall was huge and darkly paneled, dominated by an enormous fireplace that was crackling furiously, sending upward a shower of sparks. A picture of a knight in armor was hung above the projecting mantle, its frame adorned with bright red-berried holly. There were other baronial touches here and there—a suit of burnished armor in one corner, a pair of enormous antlers hung on the wall, several cumbersome pieces of furniture that had defied the ages. At first, Jemima concluded, the company looked incongruous in this medieval setting. But then she modified her impression: this company would have looked incongruous anywhere.

Like most branches of any large, wide-flung family, they were a varied lot, made up of a profusion of ancient aunts and uncles, comfortable matrons with portly spouses, superannuated spinsters, blooming debutantes, and several jubilant escapees from boarding school. Their evening clothes ran the gamut from fairly modish to genteel shabby, testifying to an uneven distribution of worldly goods. Jemima felt relieved that she was in no danger of being put to the blush by her own white crepe round dress, despite the fact it stood in some need of a smoothing iron.

This uncharacteristic self-consciousness caused her to seek out its source. And it didn't take long to spot Lord Montague. She only needed to follow the gazes of all the females present (and the majority of the men) to see him standing in comfortable range of the roaring fire, flanked by her aunt and cousin, one gushing while the other fawned.

Jemima was unworthily pleased to see that his lordship's understated elegance showed up her cousin for the popinjay he was. Perhaps if they're half as friendly as Marcus imagines, he can get the name of the odious viscount's tailor, she thought. She studied Montague's face again, this time with some detachment. I don't see why Aunt Lawford should label him 'Adonis,' she concluded satisfactorily. He's too . . . pokerish . . . by half. His face might be made of granite. And I'll bet a monkey he's not hearing a word that's being said, though I can hardly criticize him for that. Just then the black eyes turned her way, and she quickly gazed off in another direction.

"Can this truly be little Jemima?" A voice spoke at her elbow. "My dear, what a beautiful young lady you've become."

"Uncle Walter?"

Jemima had little memory of the stately gray-haired man beaming down at her. Deeply involved in governmental affairs, he had rarely joined his wife and son on their infrequent visits to the Chatham cottage. "I can't tell you how much it means to have my family around me in the Yuletide season," he was saying. "I'm only sorry that your mother and sisters were unable to come as well."

Jemima wondered if he labored under the illusion that her mother and sisters had been invited, but she merely smiled and refrained from comment.

"Yes, even though for the rest of the year I'm swamped with the demands of Ministry affairs and forced by town society into modern ways, I am bound and determined to keep the old values alive here at Christmastide. And your aunt," he smiled, "is forced to indulge me in my 'freaks' as Marcus terms it. Oh, Ada has her complete way with the town house. And I can assure you, it's up to the latest style. But I'm determined to keep the court the way my ancestors left it and cling to the old customs, at least for one season of the year.

"Ah now, I see that it's time to lead our guests in to dinner. But first let me present you to my sister who is most eager to make your acquaintance. Oh

Jane, m'dear," he called to disengage a lady from the center of a chatting group. She turned and smiled and then came toward them.

At first Jemima hardly knew which way to look, for it was painful to watch the lady's progress. She was afflicted with a limp that bordered on the grotesque, causing her to bob up and down and twist her body awkwardly in order to gain forward momentum. But once Jemima's eyes had traveled to her face, she forgot all about the unfortunate deformity. Miss Jane Lawford was possessed of her brother's sweet expression, clear gray eyes, and handsome features. Though she wore a cap over her light brown curls, Jemima wondered if she were old enough to be required to do so.

Sir Walter must have read her mind. "Jane is my baby sister," he explained after he'd presented the ladies to one another. "We are the eldest and youngest of an extensive brood with twenty years between us. Now I shall have to leave you two young ladies, for my wife has been trying to attract my attention for several minutes."

During their necessarily slow progress into the dining room, Jemima learned that Miss Lawford was acting mistress of the court. "I have lived here all my life," she explained, "and I not only know the servants well but also their families and their histories. And your aunt is here so rarely, it seems fitting that when she does come she be allowed a holiday from household cares."

Jemima thought that a most tactful way to excuse her aunt's indolence. Her respect for Miss Lawford increased.

Like the great hall, the enormous dining chamber was paneled in heavy oak that gleamed from polishing. Portraits of Lawford ancestors ringed these walls, their stern appearance lightened by the holly and the ivy that adorned them. A ponderous buffet took up a large portion of one wall. Among the family plate stood two tall Christmas candles surrounded by cheerful greenery.

Except in the case of Lord Montague, who was accorded the place of honor, the seating arrangement was quite informal. Jemima was happy when Miss Lawford led them to a place in the center of the lengthy, heavy oaken table where they were comfortably removed from her aunt and cousin. The table was lavishly spread with the first remove. "My goodness," Jemima exclaimed as she looked at the array. "Whatever will Christmas itself be like?"

"Well you can rely on one thing," the chubby-cheeked middle-aged gentleman next to her chuckled. "It will be traditional."

Across the table from them Miss Lawford made the introductions. The gentleman was identified as Dr. Jackson. "He keeps us healthy," she explained.

"Now that is a blatant whisker. The truth of the matter is, Miss Forbes, that Miss Lawford here is my greatest rival. She's the one who concocts all sorts of medicines from the herbs she gathers or grows herself, prescribes the remedies, and sees to the dosing. I vow she'll run me out of business yet, for most of my patients only come to me when she insists upon it. I'm only waiting for her to charge a fee," he laughed, "to shut down her practice. But since she refuses compensation for her services, I may have to resort to accusing her of witchcraft."

"Pay him no heed, Miss Forbes. Dr. Jackson is a shameless wag, as you'll soon discover."

"No, it's true, young lady." The physician turned serious. "Miss Lawford is far too modest. She is a truly gifted healer. With her, medicine is an art. While I'm a mere practitioner, a man of science."

"He does exaggerate," Miss Lawford smiled. "But before I change the subject, which I'm quite determined to do, I must tell you, Miss Forbes, that your maid—Bess, is she not called?—has just broken out in spots."

"Oh no, the measles! Two of my sisters were infected, but Bess was quite sure she'd had them, as I have, or I'd never have permitted her to come."

Jemima glanced uneasily down the table at her aunt, who could hardly eat her dinner for keeping her eyes fastened upon Lord Montague, monitoring his fork's every move from plate to mouth. Just how that formidable lady would react to the fact that her unwelcome niece had brought the measles into her household didn't bear thinking on.

Miss Lawford appeared to read her mind. "I see no reason to worry my sister-in-law with such a minor domestic matter. Most, if not all the servants, have already had them. And Bess does not appear to be inordinately ill. But you will take a look at her, won't you, Doctor?"

"Very well. But only to keep up appearances, mind you. For you will have already done everything necessary for the patient. I'll stake my life on that."

The doctor then turned to converse with the lady on his other side, giving Jemima the opportunity to scan the forty or so guests gathered at the table. Just where in this assembly was the young man who'd been invited for Clarissa? There was not much to choose from. The two Oxionians were surely too callow to be considered. As for the four of five gentlemen present who ranged from early to late middle age, she suspected that they came equipped with wives.

In fact the only person who seemed to qualify in terms of age and bachelorhood was Lord Montague. And he'd been ruled out in no uncertain terms. Which was just as well. She for one was not impressed by his rank and fortune. She looked for far more in a gentleman than that. Not that she was apt to find him among this group. Her eyes swept the table again while she sighed inadvertently. His lordship intercepted her gaze with a level look. To her intense disgust, Jemima felt her face grow red.

Chapter Five

JEMIMA STAYED BY Miss Lawford's side as the ladies left the dining chamber, for she was convinced she would find no more congenial person at the court. Further conversation in the withdrawing room confirmed her impression. She found her uncle's sister to be an interesting conversationalist, possessed of an intelligent dry wit that was completely free of spitefulness. However, when the gentlemen rejoined the ladies, Miss Lawford tried to discourage Jemima from accompanying her to a whist table. "There's to be dancing, you know. You really should join the young people." But when Jemima demurred, pleading fatigue after her trying journey, she did not argue. Jemima suspected that she realized Lady Lawford would be best pleased if her country niece remained inconspicuous.

Lady Lawford was *not* pleased, however, when Lord Montague presented himself at their whist table and asked to join them. Her ladyship was, in fact, horrified. But all her attempts to persuade the guest of honor that the young ladies would be devastated if he did not dance met with a chilly politeness that soon routed her.

Certainly no one was more amazed than Jemima when his lordship sat down with them. Much to her relief she was not forced to partner him, for seconds earlier an octogenarian with an alarming tendency to wheeze had seated himself across from her.

Competitive by nature, she was suddenly seized by a burning desire to best his high and mighty lordship, to make him wish that he'd never wrecked *her* coach! But her hopes for even this petty revenge were soon dashed. Indeed, if Lord Montague had been playing with any other partner than Miss Lawford, she would have accused him of cheating then and there as he deftly raked in trick after trick.

She might at least have put up a spirited defense (for in her own household she was thought to be a wizard at cards) if it had not been for her inept partner. The old man's attention constantly wandered from the game, causing him to select the cards he played almost at random. Jemima had all she could do to contain her disgust. Her disposition was not sweetened by the amused look his lordship gave her when her partner inadvertently topped her winning card.

When it fell to the old gentleman's lot to play a hand, he sat and studied his cards interminably, then chose one at last only to change his mind after it had traveled slowly across the table and snatch it back to the safety of his hand. During this agonizing indecision Jemima studied Lord Montague covertly from underneath her carefully lowered lids.

Why on earth had he chosen the whist table over the dance floor? That he was bored with the entire company and wished himself in Jerico, she did not doubt. Still, reason told her, he would never normally have selected her company as a lesser evil. The truth was, she concluded, that his lordship was sickening for something. His face was pale and drawn; the lines she'd observed earlier had deepened. For one joyous, gloating moment she hoped she'd somehow infected him with Bess's measles. But, of course, that was absurd. Even if such a thing were possible, there had not been time enough. No, on closer observation she concluded that he was injured in some fashion. Certainly he was holding his cards awkwardly. Then she remembered the basin that the servant had been carrying from his room. Surely a shaving nick could not have accounted for so much blood. She scanned his face more closely while her partner once again sent a card on a round trip toward the center of the table and back into his hand again.

His lordship stared her way coldly. "Do I perhaps have gravy on my chin, Miss Forbes?"

"Er—why, no." She was mortified that he had caught her out. "I was just wondering if you're all right, that's all."

His eyebrows rose. "Should I not be? Did you hope to send me into a decline with the tongue-banging that you gave me?"

"Hardly," she rallied. "I doubt that I made the slightest impression. I just thought you might have hurt yourself, that's all. Your arm perhaps?"

"Why, no. Though I should perhaps be grateful for your concern, I confess that I'm actually rather puzzled by it. For instance, it would never occur to me that you yourself might appear to be a bit hag-ridden since I've no basis for comparison. We have only just met, you know."

Jane was looking at them rather oddly. The elderly gentleman at last made up his mind, and the play resumed.

Jemima could hardly contain her relief when the

appearance of the tea tray brought all activities to an end. She was developing the headache, she realized. That could account for his odious lordship's 'hag-ridden' remark.

Sir Walter would not allow his guests to help themselves to refreshments and then scatter throughout the room. He insisted that they all gather around the fireplace for common fellowship.

Conversation was awkward at first, which was only natural. Speaking up in such a large gathering would be a bit like addressing parliament, Jemima thought. She also suspected that the majority were intimidated by the august presence of Lord Montague.

She herself was certainly not indifferent to him. She'd been at some pains to sit as far away as possible, an ambition that met with his approval, she suspected. The ploy was only partially successful, though. Although they were indeed separated by scores of people in a semicircle formed of chairs, sofas, and footstools, they did wind up facing one another. Jemima was hard put to know just where to look.

Some neighboring squire had first cleared his throat, then ventured a few remarks concerning what weather they might expect, based on the evidence of past Christmases, when Jemima's whist partner abruptly gained the company's attention. "Oh, I say, Sir Walter," he inquired in the overloud voice of the hard of hearing, "is it true that Baldwin Hall has a new occupant?"

Since Jemima had been trying so hard not to look at Lord Montague, of course her eyes were glued upon him when the question was asked. She did not imagine his reaction, she told herself afterward. For the briefest instant, his lordship had looked stunned.

Her curiosity was aroused even further when she felt Miss Lawford, seated beside her, stiffen. And even Sir Walter seemed to have been made uncomfortable by the question. "I think I did hear something of the sort," he said dismissively. "Now shall we—"

"Deuced odd, when you stop to think on it." The ancient seemed unaware he was interrupting as he held forth in his tinny voice. "An estate that's been in one family since God knows how long—back to the Conqueror, it wouldn't surprise me—suddenly gets passed around like a red-hot coal. Wonderful, I'd call it."

"Well, actually," another gentleman, who'd been identified to Jemima earlier as Sir Walter's cousin several times removed, spoke up, "it's not being passed around, so I understand. It's reverting. By hook or crook, Edward Baldwin's managed to buy it back."

This time there was no mistaking a dropped bombshell. Or teacup, to be more precise. For Miss Lawford's, fortunately empty, shattered upon the floor.

Chapter Six

WHILE A FOOTMAN leaped to retrieve the shattered shards of china, a white-faced Miss Lawford murmured her apologies. Jemima also noticed that the well-informed cousin was receiving a whispered tongue-lashing from his wife.

Sir Walter tried to restore a festive spirit with a rather too hearty suggestion that they tell ghost stories. This notion was met with embarrassed protests from his wife and son. They in turn were interrupted by the butler who appeared in the doorway, clearing his throat. "Mr. Lloyd Newbright has just arrived," he announced.

All eyes turned toward the entryway where a personable young man dressed in riding coat and buckskins was standing. He appeared to be in his late twenties with light brown hair and keen blue eyes that scanned the assembly. *Oh, I say*, Jemima thought as the eyes lingered on her for just a moment, *this must be Clarissa's young man*. Christmas, of a sudden, seemed a lot more promising.

Sir Walter hurried to clasp the newcomer by the hand and usher him toward the fire. "Lloyd, my boy. We were worried about you. Thought you'd have been here hours ago. I trust you had no trouble.

"Pray allow me to present my secretary to those of

you who haven't made his acquaintance. My *invaluable* secretary, I might add, Mr. Newbright. I'll not present the entire company to you just yet, Lloyd. I will, however, make you known to our honored guest, Lord Montague."

"Actually, we're acquainted," his lordship supplied. The two gentlemen nodded to one another, none too cordially. This lack of warmth raised the newcomer's standing in Jemima's eyes.

"And did you just arrive as well, Montague?" Mr. Newbright asked.

"Good gad, no. I've been here donkey's years," the other drawled. "Why do you ask?"

"Simple curiosity, I collect."

Mr. Newbright turned to his host once more. "I do apologize for being late, Sir Walter. And, no, I had no difficulty on the road. Actually made the journey in record time. The fact is, I was delayed by events in London that I wish to share. But first might I partake of the bounty of your tea board? For I must own I'm famished since I did not wish to delay my arrival further by stopping long enough to eat."

The majority of the company seemed indifferent to whatever might have taken place in London and drifted, yawning, off to bed. Jemima, however, was not in the least bit sleepy. She helped herself to more tea and took a chair within easy earshot of Mr. Newbright.

That gentleman seemed to enjoy building suspense, for he limited his conversation to the merest trivialities till he'd polished off the last crumb of plum cake. "Now then, Lloyd," his employer prodded, "tell us what has happened. I trust that the Regent's well. Or else," he added rather dryly, "you would have spoken sooner."

"No bodily harm has come to him, if that, as I collect, is what you mean. But his frame of mind cannot be of the best." He paused significantly.

"Oh, for heaven's sake, lad, get on with it."

Jemima silently echoed Sir Walter's sentiments. She was finding this personable young man disappointingly prosy.

"Well, sir, what I meant about the Regent's state of mind is that he cannot be best pleased that Jonathan West has been rescued."

It was a bad night for teacups. Jemima's rattled in her saucer. "Jonathan West!" she exclaimed. All eyes turned toward her. "Jonathan West the journalist?"

"Why, yes." Mr. Newbright appeared rather piqued to have been robbed of attention. "Do you know him?"

"Oh, indeed. That is to say, no, not precisely."

"Well, that certainly clears that up," Marcus observed nastily.

"Why on earth did Mr. West need to be rescued?" Jemima persisted. "And from what?"

"Oh, for God's sake, Jemima," her cousin groaned. "Where have you been for the last fortnight?"

"I'm rather amazed myself that you need to ask." Mr. Newbright recaptured the floor. "It has been the *on-dit* of London ever since Mr. West made a scurrilous attack upon the Regent in his periodical and was—rightly—arrested for it."

"Well, as for that, Lloyd," Sir Walter said mildly, "a lot of the Prince's most loyal supporters, myself included, felt he reacted too hastily. And none too wisely, I might add."

"But, sir, His Highness could not allow—"

"Oh, I say, Newbright," Lord Montague stifled a

yawn, "are you going to tell us what happened or should we go to bed and hope to read it in the *Gazette* tomorrow or whenever it happens to hit the provinces."

"I am doing so," the other glared. "To continue—what happened is simply this. Before dawn, as West was being transferred from Newgate to the prison ship that would take him to Botany Bay, his carriage was held up by a man armed with pistols who demanded that the guards release their prisoner, which the cravens did. The two then dashed off into a nearby thieve's kitchen and got away."

"My word, what an astounding story!" Sir Walter exclaimed. "Just one man, you say? Surely the prisoner was heavily guarded."

"There were three men with him. And you may be sure they were questioned over and over. But their story was that the gunman took them completely by surprise and had his pistol at the coachman's temple before they were aware of what was happening. It seems," he said dryly, "they were not prepared to die in the execution of their duty."

"I still don't understand just what Mr. West did that was so terrible," Jemima interposed. "I thought the *Orpheus* was a literary periodical."

"The problem appears to be that West himself doesn't seem to know what sort of rag he's publishing," Mr. Newbright sneered. "He should have stuck to his poetic claptrap."

"The *Orpheus*'s poems are not claptrap!"

"Some of yours, perhaps, Miss Forbes?" Lord Montague's formerly bored expression had been supplanted by a broad grin.

"No. My sister's actually," she spit back. "And they are quite superior. Everyone says so. Including

Mr. West, and he should know. He publishes some of our finest poets."

"Clarissa is a bluestocking?" Marcus appeared shocked to the soles of his evening slippers. "Well, it only needed that. Comes of a gaggle of females being reared without a man around, I collect."

"It comes of being intelligent and talented," his cousin retorted.

"I'm in no position to judge the quality of the *Orpheus*'s literary offerings," Mr. Newbright intervened. "But I do know that West's attack upon the Regent was scurrilous. Scurrilous and treasonable. And so the courts found it." The last was for Sir Walter's benefit.

"I still contend," that gentleman replied mildly, "that the Regent—or the courts, perhaps I should better say—overreacted. While I agree that holding the acting monarch up to ridicule is in the poorest possible taste, still,this is England. And even setting aside the issue of free speech, the whole matter would have best been ignored for other reasons. The *Orpheus*, after all, has a rather small, though," he smiled at his niece, "*select* circulation, and even among these few readers, I daresay the piece would have been soon forgotten. But, as it is now, the whole matter has been blown well out of proportion. Mr. West has been made a martyr. And as if all the gossip whirling around the royal marriage were not enough, with the entire populace taking sides and most of the common folk siding with Caroline, now this business, I fear, has sunk His Highness's popularity to an all-time low. As I have said, I think he would have been well-advised to have simply ignored the libel. But since he did not, I own I think it would have been best to have given Mr. West a mere rap upon the knuckles, as it were. Deportation to Botany Bay hardly fits the crime."

Miss Jane Lawford seconded her brother. "I would have thought," she said, "that the Prince would not have so soon forgot all the criticism he received when the Hunts were jailed for a similar offense."

"But that is just the point, Miss Jane," Mr. Newbright pounced. "When the Hunts attacked his Royal Highness in print, they received, as your brother so graphically puts it, a mere knuckle rap."

"Oh, come now," Sir Walter countered. "I'd hardly call two years in prison and a large fine a 'knuckle rap.' "

" 'Prison,' sir? Leigh Hunt was given a room that was decorated like some courtesan's bower. I beg pardon, ladies, for such plain speaking, but I find it hard to contain my disgust. Mr. Hunt was not only allowed to entertain his friends but to continue publishing his rag as well. It's no wonder that the Regent insisted upon stronger measures this time. If England is to remain England, proper respect must be paid the monarchy."

"But surely that's more up to them than us," Jemima blurted, then could have bitten her tongue as Mr. Newbright bent a pained glance upon her. Too late she recalled all her mother's admonitions concerning civility.

"You'd better watch Miss Forbes, Newbright," his lordship chuckled. "She has definite republican leanings. Why earlier this very day she was naming me as a candidate for the guillotine.'

Thank you very much, Lord Montague, Jemima said silently with a speaking look. Whatever slim hope she'd had of making a favorable impression upon Clarissa's young gentleman was clearly lost forever.

"Well, it's all a bad business." Sir Walter sighed. "I do hope that now Mr. West's escaped it will all be soon forgot. I still can't help but believe that His Highness may be just as glad to see the matter end this way."

"Begging your pardon, sir, but I don't think it has ended. There's an intensive manhunt taking place right now for West *and* his rescuer. No, they'll not get away. I'd stake my reputation on it.

"In fact," he swelled with pride, "one reason for my delay is that I was summoned to Bow Street and asked to make inquiries in this neighborhood. It was known I was coming here, you see, and since the fugitives are almost certain to be trying to board ship in Dover—which, by the by, will be simply crawling with king's men by now—the authorities felt it a good idea that I nose around a bit. You see, they did come up with one important bit of information. It seems that two 'toffs,' as they were termed, were seen driving near the dock area as if the very devil were after them."

"Well if two gentlemen were fool enough to venture into that neighborhood, why then I expect he was," Marcus observed. "Wouldn't catch me going there. Especially at that hour."

"That's my point exactly. It was a most unusual circumstance. But the thing is, they gave a very good description of the rig. Quite 'flash,' they called it. Shiny black and red." He cut his eyes his lordship's way. "By the by, Montague, don't you have a curricle like that?"

"Yes, as a matter of fact. I've had it for over a

year now. Which means it's been copied by at least a dozen coves. I've been thinking seriously of getting rid of it. I say, Marcus, you wouldn't be interested in taking it off my hands, would you?"

Mr. Lawford did not answer. He was too engaged with glaring at his father's secretary. "Well now, really, Newbright," he blustered. "You surely aren't trying to connect Monty with this business. Why that's . . . that's . . . preposterous!"

"Preposterous? Isn't that coming it a bit too strong? You are a good friend of Mr. West's are you not, Lord Montague?"

His lordship took a while to mull the question over. "No," he finally answered, "I'd not say I was a *good* friend. Much more than an acquaintance, certainly. For we went all through school together. But the thing is, we hadn't much else in common. I didn't—like Miss Forbes here—share Jonathan's poetic—or political—leanings. I was more into games, actually."

"I can tell you right now, Newbright, I don't care much for your insinuations," Marcus fumed. "You've no right to insult my guest under my own roof, sir."

"Softly, Marcus," his father intervened while the others present hardly knew which way to look. "There's no need to go off half-cocked. I'm sure that Lloyd was not implying—"

"And even if he were," his lordship chuckled suddenly, "damn if I'm not flattered. One cove, you say, held up a coach that was bristling with guards?"

"I did not say 'bristling.' There were merely three, in fact."

"Still, that's rather impressive. But, no, sorry to disappoint you, old man. I couldn't be two places at once, now could I?"

"You don't disappoint me, for Sir Walter is quite right; I wasn't making any accusations. I know perfectly well that you could not have been involved." In spite of his disclaimer, Mr. Newbright did look quite regretful. "For not only, if you say so, is the timing wrong, the more telling thing is," he paused dramatically, "that the man who rescued Jonathan West was shot."

This time Jemima did actually drop her teacup.

Chapter Seven

JEMIMA TOSSED AND turned all through the night. A great deal of the time was spent in upbraiding herself for being fanciful. It was absurd to think that Lord Montague had anything to do with that crime in London. Just because she didn't care for him above half was no reason to cast him in the role of arch villain.

Still though, she flopped over on her stomach trying to find a more comfortable position, the very reason she had taken against him certainly fit the circumstances. He had been riding hell-bent down the Dover Road, putting all chance travelers in peril of their lives. And unless she'd missed her calculations, it *was* possible for him to have been in London at the fateful hour. He'd certainly given Mr. Newbright a false impression about his arrival time. Of that she was sure. But most damning of all was the matter of the bloody basin. Not to mention the way he seemed to be protective of his left arm. No indeed, this was not mere fancy. Lord Montague was guilty as sin and she could prove it!

But guilty of what? Of rescuing a friend, or an acquaintance, from a harshly unjust sentence. Some might even call that heroism.

"Fustian!" Jemima muttered into her pillow. Her

thoughts were really getting out of hand. She might have been too quick to pronounce his lordship guilty based on some rather flimsy evidence and a strong dislike, but now to label him a 'hero'? That was downright sap-skulled.

A pox on his lordship, anyhow. Jonathan West was her real concern. Or more accurately, her sister's reaction to his fate.

She had teased Clarissa unmercifully about being in love with the journalist. Her sister had indignantly denied the accusation. "Of course I'm not in love with him. How could I be in love with someone I've never even met? Really, Jemima, you are absurd. Oh, I don't mind saying that I enjoy our correspondence. It's wonderful to find I've so much in common with an intellectual like Mr. West."

Well, Jemima flip-flopped in bed again, perhaps he could continue his correspondence from France. That is, if he ever got there. Judging by what Mr. Newbright had said, his chances were slim indeed. Blast the man, anyhow! Why had he taken it upon himself to lambaste his Royal Highness? Prinny already had detractors enough and to spare in the kingdom. Mr. West could just as well have filled up his space with another of Clarissa's poems. Jemima fell asleep at last only to dream of her timid older sister planted in the middle of the highway, pistols cocked, shouting "Stand and deliver!" at a black and red curricle that was bearing down upon her.

When Jemima was roused next morning by the sounds of the window curtains being pulled, she could have sworn she'd never closed her eyes. She sat up and gratefully sipped the steaming cup of tea the maid had brought her. Then, after first checking on Bess and finding her a riot of spots but reasonably content and well cared for, she decided that a walk before breakfast might help clear the cobwebs from the brain.

Striding rapidly in the icy air, she followed a path that led toward the stables. She was eager to inspect her uncle's cattle. Perhaps there'd be an opportunity later on to ride.

Jemima was distracted from her mission, though, by the sound of piteous mewing. She paused to listen, then left the path to track the heart-wrenching sounds to their source. As she forced her way through the thick hedge that lined the path, Jemima was astonished to see Lord Montague standing at the base of an enormous beech tree, staring up into its branches. "What are you doing out so early?" she blurted.

If he was startled by her sudden materialization he hid it well. "And should I not be?" He eyed her stonily. "Are decadent noblemen required to stay in bed till noon?"

"Perhaps you were too uncomfortable to sleep," she countered.

"Why, no. I agree that the Court's accommodations are a bit primitive, but my bed is adequate. I take it, then, that you fared worse?"

"That wasn't what I meant, and you know it. I thought perhaps you might be in pain."

"No. Sorry to disapepoint you, but I'm quite well. A touch of dyspepsia, perhaps, from last night's shellfish. But other than that—"

They were interrupted by a renewal of the pathetic mewing that had abated for a moment upon her arrival.

"What on earth?" Jemima moved closer to gaze up into the bare branches. The tiny ball of fluff clinging to the trunk about halfway up was difficult to spot, so closely did its gray coloring match the wood it clung to. "Why the poor thing. It's afraid to come down."

"A brilliant deduction, Miss Forbes."

She wheeled accusingly. "Did you frighten the poor little thing up there?"

"Well, naturally. I was feeling a bit bored you understand, what with no coaches to run off the road, so I said to myself, 'By Jove, Monty, why not go chase a kitten up a tree?' "

"No need to be sarcastic. Have you tried to coax it down?"

"As a matter of fact, I only just arrived. But I rather doubt my powers of persuasion."

"Here puss, puss, puss," Jemima cajoled, holding up her arms tenderly. "Come on. I'll catch you."

The only answer was a plaintive mew followed by a derisive chuckle from his lordship.

She turned and looked at him coldly. "Well it's perfectly obvious, isn't it? Someone will have to climb up and rescue the poor little thing."

"It's not obvious to me. Cats have been going up and down trees since Noah with no help from humankind. It will come down as soon as we leave, I'll wager."

"How can you be so unfeeling?" The kitten added its concurrence to this sentiment by increasing the level of anguish in its cries. "You should go up after it, you know." She paused then to give him a knowing look. "But of course you can't, now can you? You've hurt yourself."

"Why, no. And why this odd obsession with my health? The reason, one at any rate, that I've no plans to shinny up that tree is that I've no intention of ruining a pair of biscuit pantaloons."

"Well, in that case I'll simply have to do it myself."

"Do you know what I've always found to be the most objectionable thing about your sex, Miss Forbes? Your complete inability to look at an issue rationally. You wish me to climb a tree after a cat. I refuse to do anything so blatantly idiotic, and your reaction is that you'll have to do it yourself. Any fool would perceive that there are several alternatives to that pea-brained bit of action. But since your real objective is not a kitten rescue but a desire to shame me—which I can assure you you'll not achieve—then don't let me stop you. Miss Forbes," he made a sweeping gesture toward the beech, "the tree."

She looked at it doubtfully. She had not climbed a tree since she was twelve, and then she had not been wearing her best French gray round dress with a cherry-colored spenser.

"Having second thoughts?" he jeered.

"No. I am simply waiting for you to leave."

"So you can fetch the gardener?"

Blast the man, he'd read her mind. "Certainly not. I have no need of a gardener." She spoke with more bravado than she was feeling. "Nor do I require an audience. If you aren't going to help, at least take yourself off."

"And miss your demonstration? Never. Why, who knows. I may at some future date be moved to stage a feline rescue myself, and I'll not shirk this opportunity to master the technique."

He'd called her bluff. Trying not to grind her teeth, Jemima turned back to size up the situation. As she peered up among the branches, the kitten peered back down at her. Its mew was even more pathetic than before.

Well, there was no turning back at this point. She reached up to clasp the lowest branch. It was barely out of reach. She jumped for it and managed to grab hold but did not quite see how best to proceed from there. As she dangled, swaying ridiculously to and fro, she would have given a great deal to be wearing the biscuit pantaloons his lordship was so carefully preserving.

As she dropped back to the ground, she heard a muffled chuckle. "Instead of laughing like an ill-mannered hyena, you might give me a boost, you know."

"Oh no, not I. Break your neck if you insist, but I'll be no party to it."

Jemima had been so preoccupied with the kitten's plight that she'd momentarily forgot her suspicions. They returned, full force. "You don't really care a fig whether I break my neck or not. You simply aren't able to lift me."

"Hmm." He measured her carefully with his eyes. "You think not? Oh, I've probably lifted heavier females in my time."

"You know perfectly well what I mean. You can't do it—any more than you can climb this tree—because you're hurt."

He shook his head pityingly. "God knows what maggots you have in your brain, Miss Forbes, but I can assure you that I'm perfectly sound of body. And if you're bound and determined to commit suicide over a cat, well then, here goes." Before she realized his intention she was suddenly shot aloft to land on her posterior upon the branch. It was all she could do to keep from tumbling over backward, let alone determine whether he'd managed to propel her skyward by the use of only one arm or two.

"Well, thank you very much," she gasped after she'd established some equilibrium. "You may leave now."

"Not I. I'll just stand here and admire the limbs. Of the tree, naturally."

It was bad enough having to climb a tree hampered by skirts without modesty also being a consideration. But Jemima did her best, staying close to the trunk and proceeding carefully. She did appreciate the fact that the beech was ideal for climbing. Its branches grew close together, providing ample footage. After inching herself upward for several feet without encountering any problems, she looked down to register her contempt for his lordship's cravenness. And instantly regretted it. She gasped and froze.

"Never look down, Miss Forbes," he called. "That was the kitten's mistake. I shudder to think of both of you being stranded up there."

She gritted her teeth and tried to think of more pleasant things than plummeting to earth. Wiping the smirk off Lord Montague's face sprang instantly to mind.

Once the giddiness had passed she resumed her upward climb while the kitten watched with considerable interest, its green eyes wide. "Here puss, puss, puss," she crooned soothingly. "Hang on, dear. Jemima will get you down."

She was near enough now to make it feasible to reach out and clasp the little thing. The problem was, she had not worked out the logistics of this maneuver. Releasing a hand from the limb she clutched like grim death seemed unthinkably foolhardy. And how on earth was she to manage her descent while gripping a kitten? Well, surely the cat could cling to her shoulder and leave both her hands free. That was little enough to ask, considering.

"Here puss, puss, puss, get ready for a ride," she said in a bracing tone. And clasping one arm around the tree trunk, she stretched the other hand toward it. The kitten gave the grasping fingers a horrified look, then scrambled farther up the tree to safety, where it increased its howling.

"Oh, blast!"

"Did you say something, Miss Forbes?"

"Oh, do be quiet. Your shouting's scaring the little thing."

"I'm scaring the little thing! It seems to me it's you that's put the little ingrate in a quake. Give it up and come on down. It's my opinion that those upper branches won't bear your weight. No offense intended, I assure you. You were, of course, the merest feather when I gave you that boost."

Jemima was not listening. A flash of movement in the near distance had caught her eye. The hedge she'd come through when she'd first responded to the catcalls was rustling. Her first thought was that a wind had just sprung up and all that was needed was for her to be whipped around in the heights like some schoolmaster's switch.

She clutched the tree tighter but felt no movement from it. Risking another look, she noted with relief that her head was losing some of its tendency to swim. And the movement of the hedge was not caused, she now discovered, by an act of nature but by human intervention. Someone was crouched next to it, parting the branches in order to peer through. On closer examination that 'someone' was Mr. Newbright. And his crouching position looked not only odd but furtive. He was spying upon Lord Montague.

"Pray tell me you're not frozen up there again," the object of Mr. Newbright's attention called to Jemima. "Do give it up and come on down. That imbecile cat will eventually discover that it can travel down as well as up. You've proven your point. I declare myself positively overcome by your heroism. Or heroineism. Is there such a word? Damned if I know," he reflected. "Can't say as the question has ever come up before."

Jemima decided to follow this recommended course of action. Not because of his lordship's powers of persuasion, needless to say. Rather she found something a bit sinister in Mr. Newbright's surveillance and felt it only sporting that Lord Montague be made aware of it.

She therefore proceeded back down the tree with more alacrity than she'd employed on her upward climb. Indeed, distracted by this new preoccupation, she abandoned the cautionary measure of carefully testing each branch before putting her weight on it.

"Watch that limb!"

His lordship's warning had come too late. There was a blood-chilling crack. Then Jemima came hurtling downward.

"Oof!"

Lord Montague had managed to break her fall, but the two were borne to the ground by the impact of it. Jemima lay sprawled atop him trying to determine if she were alive or dead. Once her own survival had been established, her more unselfish instincts surfaced. She raised her head to stare into his lordship's glassy eyes. "Oh, my heavens, are you quite all right?"

"What a damn-fool question. Now for God's sake would you get off me."

Jemima quickly complied, too alarmed to take offense. She knelt beside him, peering anxiously at his chalk-white face. "Do you think anything is broken?"

"I doubt it. You just knocked the wind out of me, that's all."

"Here now. Let me help you up."

Without thinking she clasped his wrists and began to tug. This action produced a cry of pain. "Stop it, you numbskull. Do you want to kill me?"

"Oh, my heavens. I am sorry. Don't move. I'll get help."

She was about to shout for Mr. Newbright when Lord Montague said faintly, "No need of that. I'm quite all right. Sorry to have snapped your head off." He pushed himself into a sitting position and leaned back against the tree trunk. "Just let me catch my breath, and I'll be fit as your average fiddle."

"That I doubt. You look like warmed-over death, to speak quite plainly. While I was up in the tree I saw Mr. Newbright on the path. Let me go fetch him. Frankly I'm amazed he hasn't come of his own accord. I'm certain he was looking this way."

"Undoubtedly. He's been following me all morning. But I don't think he'll wish to put in an appearance."

"Well how very pecul— Oh, my heavens!" She stared at his left hand in horror. A dark red trickle was running down from under his coat sleeve. "You're bleeding! Oh I will have to go for help."

"The devil you will. Here, lean a bit closer, will you. Damned if I seem to have the strength of that benighted kitten."

She obligingly complied, thinking it would be heartless to question a man who might bleed to death before her very eyes. Then, with surprising strength for one hovering on the brink, his lordship pulled her tight against his chest.

"What *are* you doing?" she gazed up to demand as he bent his head to kiss her. She was too astonished by this development to think of extracting herself from such a shocking intimacy. Then, after a bit, when the issue of propriety did niggle, it seemed best to humor a man who might well succumb to the Grim Reaper at any moment.

But when he at last released her and she had caught her breath, her sensibilities sorted themselves sufficiently for her to glare at him. His lordship appeared unable to meet her eyes. Shame, she had supposed, till he leaned back against the tree trunk and began to chuckle.

Why that shameless, decadent, lecherous . . . that . . . that viscount! How dare he find amusement in the fact that she'd so easily given in to his improper advances. If he thought for one minute! But then she followed the direction of his gaze. "Oh, of all the—"

The kitten was lying on the frosty grass licking its paws, surveying them with interest.

"Forgive me if I say 'I told you so.' "

"Perhaps," she replied icily, "you might instead explain just what that last business was all about, Lord Montague. Am I now supposed to be so smitten that I don't tell Mr. Newbright that what he suspected all along is true?"

"Why, no, Miss Forbes. What I had hoped to accomplish was to avoid the necessity of speaking to Mr. Newbright at all. And to provide a reason for us to walk very closely together back to the court. For, to tell the truth, I don't think I can manage it on my own."

He saw her hesitation. "Oh, come, Miss Forbes. There are other explanations of my injury besides the one that Mr. Newbright suggested. An irate husband for instance. Oh, very well then. Since I doubt I could convince Newbright of that, either, I'd just as soon avoid a confrontation. Couldn't you wrestle with your conscience later? It's not as if I'll be going anywhere, you know."

He struggled to his feet, swaying slightly. Jemima jumped up to steady him, then realized that to any interested onlooker it would appear like a second embrace. "Oh, blast!" she muttered and he grinned feebly. "Oh, well. Come on, then, I'll help you."

They started toward the house pressed against each other like a pair of lovers, her arm around his waist and his resting heavily upon her shoulder. She was relieved to see that the bleeding appeared to have stopped.

When they gained the path she risked a peek behind her. There was no sight of Mr. Newbright. "He's gone," she whispered.

"No, he merely crept around to the other side of the hedge when we came through it. We're still under surveillance, so hang on for just a little bit longer."

"Oh? You have eyes in the back of your head, then? Well, I'll wager you that Mr. Newbright has been toasting by the fire for a good half hour."

"And I just made up that story as an excuse for intimacy? Well, if it pleases you to think so—"

"It does nothing of the kind!" she snapped, and they proceeded on in silence.

As soon as they came in sight of Lawford Court,

though, his lordship stopped using her for a crutch. "I collect I can make it on my own now. No need to ruin your character."

I'd say you've already done that," she answered glumly.

"With Newbright? You surely can't care what that self-important cit might think. Oh, I forgot. According to Marcus, the plan was to throw you at his head. Well believe me, Miss Forbes, you are far better off."

"Oh, you think so? Well, I should have preferred to make that determination for myself. Here, where are you going now?"

"The servant's entrance. It's the shortest route to my bedchamber. This is where we part company, Miss Forbes."

"As much as that state of affairs appeals to me, I doubt you can make it on your own."

"I'm sure I can. Good day, Miss Forbes."

"That's it? Good day?"

"What else? Surely you aren't suggesting that we kiss again?"

"That odious remark was quite uncalled for. What I had thought, your lordship, was that a word of thanks might have been in order. But I can see that I mistook the matter."

"Thanks? For what? Falling on top of me? No, of course not. You mean for supporting me this far. Well, I am grateful, Miss Forbes. It's just that I didn't wish to waste valuable time in chatter."

"Chatter? Well I'd not call simple civility 'chatter.' But don't let me detain you further. Good day, Lord Montague."

"And good riddance," she muttered to herself as she watched his slow and slightly unsteady progress toward the house.

Chapter Eight

Oh, there you are, Jemima." Sir Walter beamed as his niece entered the dining chamber. "Come and join me. I think we're among the last at breakfast. Though I understand his lordship has yet to appear. And, as for Marcus," he grimmaced with distaste, "he rarely rises before noon. Do help yourself from the sideboard, m'dear. We breakfast quite informally."

The morning's events had left her ravenous. She piled her plate liberally with Sally Lund, beef ribs, and a boiled egg, then went to join her uncle. The oak table had seemed large the night before; it now seemed enormous.

"Have you been walking?" Sir Walter asked, and Jemima, her mouth full, merely nodded. "My sister was looking for you earlier. She has gone to take some baby garments to one of our tenants and thought you might have liked to go along and see something of the countryside."

"Oh, I should have done," Jemima said regretfully.

"Never mind. We shall see to it that you get a tour. It's our pride to show it off, you see. For we think that this part of England is exceptional, even in midwinter. My sister is particularly eager to be your guide. She likes you very much, Jemima."

"And I her," his niece replied sincerely.

"I'm glad of that. For I fear that Jane leads a very lonely life. Though she hides it well, she is quite self-conscious about her infirmity and inclined to remain reclusive."

"She should not be," Jemima protested. "Oh, I own that it is what one notices most particularly at first, but then one forgets all about it immediately."

"I'm pleased to hear you say so, m'dear. For I don't think it's prejudice on my part when I say that except for the one flaw my sister is one of the finest examples of her sex. Unfortunately it speaks ill of my own sex that her physical deformity has put her outside the pale for marriage."

"I don't see why. She's intelligent . . . witty . . . kind . . ."

"You are quite right, of course." Sir Walter spoke dryly. "Unfortunately those are not the qualities that men look for first and foremost in a lady."

"Well, they should!"

"Oh, I quite agree," he smiled and then turned serious once more. "Jane has one asset, however, that can attract a certain unscrupulous type of man. She has inherited quite a substantial income. And several years ago I was forced to scotch a planned elopement with a scoundrel who was a blatant fortune hunter. There was no doubt whatsoever on that score. He cared for nothing except her fortune. He'd run through his own inheritance, you see. Gambled it away. And I could not stand by and allow the same fate to overcome my sister's. So I put a stop to the whole business."

He sighed deeply. "It was the right thing to do, of course. I had no choice in the matter. Still, I sometimes wonder what might have happened if I hadn't interfered. Perhaps Jane might have had a brief period of happiness before disillusionment set in. Still, I expect I'm merely being maudlin. This season always brings with it an excess of sentiment, I fear. No, I did the right thing. There's no doubt about it."

"Does your sister blame you, sir?"

"No. Indeed, it might have been better if she had raged and railed, as most would have done. But she never uttered a single word of reproach. Poor thing. I fear the scales fell from her eyes.

"But the end result was that she seemed to draw even more into herself. Afterward I tried to have her meet some young men of the right sort who could have learned to value the qualities in Jane that you mentioned. But although she was perfectly polite, she made it quite clear that she could not return their interest." He paused to take a regretful sip of coffee and then seemed to shake off his mood.

"Forgive me, Jemima. I did not wish to give you a fit of the dismals here at this joyous season. It's just that something has come up to put Jane's welfare a great deal on my mind. And as I said, I'm delighted that she has made a new friend.

"Now then," he rubbed his hands together heartily, "just how do you intend spending the remainder of the day? Some of the ladies have retired to the morning room to do needlework and, I suspect," he chuckled, "indulge in a bit of gossip. You would perhaps care to join them?"

Jemima barely repressed a shudder, then managed to explain politely that she had no talent in either direction.

"Well then, some of our younger visitors are organizing games in the nursery, if bear-leading and Queen Ann are to your liking. Or, if you prefer more quiet pursuits, I don't mind saying that the library at Lawford Court is exceptional."

"Would you mind, sir, if I were to ride?"

"Mind? Indeed not. I shall be delighted for you to make free with my stables. But, I must own I'm amazed at your energy. First a walk, now a ride. Ah, youth!"

After Jemima had changed into her habit, she debated whether or not to check on Lord Montague. Her instincts warned her to keep her distance from that gentleman. But the Good Samaritan part of her nature replied that, odious though he might be, he was a fellow human being who could be bleeding to death, in need of assistance. As to what she should do about her almost-certain conviction that he was the guilty party who had held up the coach and released a convicted criminal, well, she counted on the ride to clear her head.

Jemima was not accustomed to indecision. However she was still debating whether to knock or not, and chiding herself for such vacillation, when his lordship's door opened in her face and she was confronted by her cousin Marcus.

"What are you doing here?" he glared.

"I'm a guest here, in case you've forgot."

"An *uninvited* guest. And how you could have the gall to come here under those circumstances is more than I can conceive of."

"Oh, for goodness sake, Marcus. Do you have to keep harping on the same old theme? I know you would have much preferred Clarissa, but there's no sense making a Cheltenham tragedy of the thing. We need have nothing to do with one another, you know."

"I'm not talking about you and me. I refer to your complete lack of consideration for others. What I fail to understand is how any right-thinking person could knowingly bring a plague upon this household."

"A plague? Oh, my heavens, Marcus, must you be so dramatic? If you're referring to Bess's case of measles, well, then I am truly sorry and would never have brought her with me if I'd known. However, I do think you're refining too much on the situation. She's well away from all your guests. And I should think your grown servants have already had the measles. Of course," she added in all honesty, "I should have thought Clarissa and Bess would have had them, too."

"That's precisely your trouble, Jemima. You don't think. I don't suppose it occurred to you that you yourself might be a carrier."

Jemima studied his stormy face and suddenly grinned. "So that's it, is it? *You* haven't had them."

"Yes, I have, as a matter of fact. But I'll tell you right now that I'd far liefer it was me."

"Far liefer than what?" She stared at the bedchamber door. "Oh, surely not."

"Yes. Most likely. For he's certainly sickening for something. And all thanks to you. Do you have any idea of what an honor it is to have Monty spend Christmas here at the Court?"

"Well, no, not really," Jemima admitted. "But it's certainly not from the want of your telling me."

"He'll never darken our door again. Not after the

shabby treatment he's received. And what are you smirking about? I'll tell you right now, there's no humor in the situation."

"Oh, but there is," she choked. "The nonesuch with measles! All broken out in spots! What will that do to his reputation?"

Chapter Nine

JEMIMA WAS STILL chuckling over the mental image of a bemeasled Lord Montague as she cantered toward the beach. The day was crisp. The air hit her lungs like needles. But even so it was grand to be out of doors. She could hardly wait for her first glimpse of the sea.

But when she reached the beach her mind proved too full of turmoil to properly appreciate the ocean's majesty. She reigned in her mount and watched the waves come pounding in. But she soon gave her mare her head again while she tried to make some sense of recent events.

A black and red curricle had been seen near the spot where Jonathan West was rescued. A black and red curricle had come speeding down the Dover Road as if the devil himself were in hot pursuit. The man who had held up the prisoner's coach had been shot. And Lord Montague was certainly not feeling quite the thing.

For a moment she entertained the notion that he actually might be coming down with measles. She recalled how miserable Clarissa had been before she blossomed. And she smiled again at the notion of his lordship similarly circumstanced. There was something so childish and undignified about measles. Humbling might do his lordship good.

But no, that was absurd. You don't bleed with measles. Lord Montague was suffering from a bullet wound, and she was the only one who knew it. The burning question was, what should she do about it?

Jemima was so absorbed with this dilemma that she galloped right past a lone man unrigging a beached fishing boat, scarcely seeing him. She was only dimly aware that he had paused in his work to stare at her. Something prodded her to glance back over her shoulder, though, whereupon she reined in her animal and rode back.

"Mr. Baldwin. How nice to see you again," she smiled as she dismounted. "I almost passed by without realizing who you were."

"Oh, well then," he smiled back and took the hand that she'd extended. "I was frankly wondering if you were avoiding me."

"Of course not. I'm still grateful for the ride you gave me."

Jemima realized that she was indeed very glad to see him. So much had happened since they'd met that he had entirely slipped her mind. But now she was reminded of how engaging she'd found him to be. And, really, he was quite nice looking in a rather shop-worn way. She caught herself wondering what he might look like after a visit to Lord Montague's tailor instead of being clad in the fisherman's knit hat, short coat, and knee breeches that he wore. "Is this your beach?" she asked, squelching that train of thought. "Am I trespassing?"

"Yes and no. You're welcome to ride here any

time." He looked admiringly at the high-mettled blond mare. "That's certainly a prime 'un."

"Yes, isn't she. She belongs to my uncle, of course."

"Sir Walter always did keep a fine stable. Are you enjoying your stay at Lawford Court, Miss Forbes?"

Jemima mulled the question seriously. "Well, I'm finding it prodigiously interesting."

He seemed to recognize the distinction. "Perhaps I shouldn't speak ill of your family, but I always did find your cousin Marcus tiresome. But then he was a mere lad when I last saw him. Perhaps he's improved with time."

"Not so as one could notice."

"Like that, is it?" he grimmaced. "Oh, well, the rest of the family surely make up for his short comings. His father is certainly one of the finest gentlemen I've ever met. And," there was a subtle alteration in his voice and expression, "does Marcus's Aunt Jane still live at the Court?"

"Oh yes. In fact, she runs the place. My aunt spends most of her time in London, you see, and is glad to pass on the responsibility. Miss Jane is marvelously capable. And a very superior person in every way. I like her prodigiously."

"She has not married then?"

"No. Which does seem a pity. At least it's supposed to seem a pity, though just why that should be is beyond my understanding. No one ever seems to pity bachelors."

"I expect that's because bachelors have more scope than spinsters do. The pity, in Miss Jane's case, I should think, is that she'd be better employed presiding over her own household than your aunt's."

"That's true. Still, the bright side is that my Aunt Ada rarely comes to Lawford Court."

He laughed at that. "I fear we've just torn both your blood relations' characters to shreds. To move the conversation to safer channels, you do have a treat in store, Miss Forbes. Sir Walter is famous, and rightly so, for his Yuletide celebrations. Keeping up the old customs is almost a religion to him. As a lad I could hardly wait each year to enjoy his hospitality."

"Yes, I understand that everyone for miles around comes to Christmas dinner."

"Well, almost everyone."

There was an awkward pause while she digested this. When they'd first met hadn't he mentioned being *persona non grata* at Lawford Court?

"Look, Miss Forbes," he interrupted her thoughts, "I had supposed you would have heard all this by now, but I seem to have overrated the gossip mongers. Or more likely still, my own importance. But the thing is, you really should not have anything more to do with me. I'm the black sheep of the neighborhood, you see. Not to wrap it in clean linen, an ex-convict."

"Oh, really?" Jemima flinched at the false brightness in her tone. To hear her, he might have just confessed he'd had a bit too much to drink the evening before. But then, what was the proper social response to such a revelation?

"Yes, really." He appeared sympathetic to her embarrassment. "You see before you the proverbial wastrel. I ran up huge gaming debts and was arrested and clapped into the Fleet for my sins. But," he shrugged, "I've served my sentence and, thanks to an inheritance, was able to buy back a good portion of the family estate. And so I've turned up again like a bad penny's supposed to."

"Then all's well that end's well, I'd say." To her own ears she still sounded like a sap-skull. But then she'd never before conversed with an ex-convict in order to practice the requisite social skills. "Surely people will be prepared to forgive and forget."

"If you think that, my dear Miss Forbes, you cannot have become acquainted with the people hereabouts. Their memories are long, believe me."

"But still," she pointed out, "while gambling is, of course, quite reprehensible, it's not on a par with say . . . murder, for instance. And given time—"

"Thank you for your encouragement. But I fear that my gambling is not the only thing held against me.

"But never mind all that. I'm thankful enough just to be here in God's country once again. I don't require the approval of my neighbors to make me a happy man. To me, 'freedom' is the most beautiful word in the English language, Miss Forbes."

"Yes, I can well imagine." Jemima was sounding more herself now. "And it must be especially gratifying to be back in your own hall."

"Well, actually, I'm living in the gate house at the moment. I fear that the ancient pile isn't fit for habitation. It's gone to rack and ruin, in point of fact. Oh, I don't take *all* the blame for that, Miss Forbes. My ancestors have been working on the decline for several generations now. You see I'm not the first of my line to be bitten by the gambling bug. Though I think I can modestly claim to have rather out done the rest." He smiled wryly. "But still, the Manor House had been decaying for donkey's years. Which no doubt is what's given it its reputation for being haunted. Ghosts seem to have an affinity for crumbling ruins. Though I've no notion why. If I were a ghost I think I'd go haunt Buck House or some other show place. But then perhaps they've no real choice in the matter."

"Your hall is haunted?" Jemima could hardly contain her delight. "I say, how famous!"

"My hall is *reported* to be haunted. I frankly always considered it a pack of nonsense. I can't believe that my ancestors would exert themselves enough to go clanging through the corridors in the dead of night. Or imagine why they should. No one was 'foully murdered,' for instance, that I ever heard of. Certainly no one ever died for love. Still, since I've been back there have been some rather strange occurrences. So don't give up hope, Miss Forbes. It could be true. God knows I hope so. Perhaps then I could charge admission and pay to have the cursed place reroofed.

"But I mustn't keep rattling on this way. It's nice to have someone to talk to, but I shouldn't keep you here. Besides the fact that someone might see you in my company, you really mustn't allow your horse to cool down this way. Here, let me help you." He knelt and made a stirrup of his hands and boosted her into the saddle. "Good-bye, Miss Forbes." He smiled his engaging smile. "Enjoy your stay at Lawford Court. And a very Merry Christmas."

Jemima had turned her horse back the way she'd come and was leaving him with a wave when he called after her. "Do give my regards . . . No, never mind. That would not be acceptable."

To Miss Jane Lawford, he was going to say, I'll bet a monkey, she thought as she rode slowly along the surf side. *For if he's not the man who tried to elope with her, then I'm a Dutchman. Well Mama was right. This visit is proving to be a broadening expe-*

rience. For I'm certainly meeting a different class of people. First a viscount who has undoubtedly committed a crime, and now a down-at-the-heels squire fresh out of prison. Why Lawford Court is a veritable Marriage Mart, I'll tell her. Almack's couldn't hope to touch it.

She clucked at her horse and picked up speed.

Chapter Ten

JEMIMA ENTERED THE court by a side entrance intending to go directly to her room. But then she decided she needed something to read and turned instead toward the library. She soon regretted the decision.

"Oh, Miss Forbes." Mr. Newbright put down the paper he was reading, pushed his chair back from the library table, and rose to his feet. "You are the very person I wish to see. You have perhaps been riding?"

"Why, yes, Mr. Newbright." *My, my, he's turning into a regular Bow Street sleuth*, was her irreverent reaction. *First skulking behind hedges, now coming up with the astounding deduction that a female dressed in riding habit has most likely been on horseback.*

But her sense of fair play soon righted itself. There was no need to be out of charity with Mr. Newbright simply because he was highly suspicious of Lord Montague and wished to see him brought to justice. When it came to that, she herself was not his lordship's greatest admirer. Besides, Mr. Newbright was a rather personable young man. And not, perhaps, as starchily prosy as he had seemed last night. She owed it to her mama—or someone—to get to know him. So when he requested a brief word with her, Jemima agreed quite civilly.

"You will perhaps judge me presumptuous, Miss Forbes, for what I'm about to say." She looked up at him curiously as he pulled out a chair for her. His face was flushed with embarrassment. "My excuse is that you are the niece of my employer and benefactor." He sat down on the opposite side of the table from her but avoided looking directly into her eyes. "Therefore, for his sake, if for no other reason, I feel compelled to speak. You may think that it would have been more the thing to have had a word with Sir Walter and allowed him to be the one to have this chat with you. But the fact of the matter is that as his secretary—and, yes, his protégé—I happen to know that he has enough distressing matters on his mind just now without bothering him with this. You do understand, don't you, Miss Forbes?"

So much for any hope she'd entertained that he might not be a prosy bore. "Why, no, Mr. Newbright, how could I possibly understand while I haven't the faintest notion of what you are talking about?"

"Ah, yes. I see. The truth is, Miss Forbes, that if I seem reluctant to come to the point it's because the matter is a very delicate one, and as I've just said, I'm not at all sure of the propriety of my being the person to speak to you."

"Oh, well then," Jemima smiled sweetly, "in that case perhaps you can recommend a book for me." Her hand gestured toward the shelves that lined the walls. "As a frequent visitor you must be well acquainted with the contents of my uncle's library. I must confess a predilection for novels. Perhaps you can suggest one?"

"No!"

"Then you do have a prejudice against novels. I feared as much. So many of your sex do, it seems. Allow me to suggest *Necromancer of the Black Forest* to you, sir. It's sure to change your opinion."

"I was not saying no to novel reading, Miss Forbes." His eyes were now riveted upon her face. "I think you choose to misunderstand me. I was saying a firm no to the notion of shirking my duty."

"Well, then, no wonder I misunderstood. The notion of your doing that never occurred to me."

"Thank you," he said stiffly, though he looked more suspicious than gratified. "Please allow me to come straight to the point, Miss Forbes."

"By all means do, Mr. Newbright."

"I wish to warn you away from Lord Montague. I think that you should know that his character—especially when it comes to dealings with the fair sex—leaves much to be desired. In fact, not to put too fine a point upon it, the man's a rakehell."

"Indeed? Well I must say I'm not in the least surprised."

He appeared nettled by her reaction. "You seem to take the news quite calmly. I do hope that, like so many silly females who become involved with gentlemen of that stamp, you aren't thinking that you'll be the one who will at last reform him and bring him to heel."

"Me?" Her eyes widened. "Bring Lord Montague to heel? I can assure you, sir, that such an absurd thought never occurred to me."

"Then frankly, Miss Forbes, I fail to see what sort of game you're playing."

"And I, Mr. Newbright, quite fail to see why you are wasting your breath with your warning. I can assure you there's no need for your concern. I find Lord Montague—and indeed all he stands for—quite odious."

"Forgive me. As much as I'd like to believe you, I fear yours is the classic case of 'the lady doth protest too much.' You see, I happen to have observed you kissing Montague."

"Oh, indeed?" He'd been so long in bringing up the matter that she'd begun to hope he'd somehow missed that episode. "Well then, did you happen to 'observe' that I fell on top of his lordship, through no fault of my own, and was hardly in any position to avoid his familiarity?"

"That all sounds very well, and I'd be inclined to accept it as a quite reasonable explanation for your shameless conduct were it not for the fact that I also observed you two walking back to the house together in a most intimate embrace."

"You saw all that? Well, then, it's wonderful to me, sir, that you did not make your presence known. Especially when I nearly broke my neck."

"I was most certainly about to do so," he flushed, "but then there was the matter of the kiss. After that, intrusion seemed . . . indelicate."

"I see." She nodded in a forgiving manner. "And I'm sure you entertained the same sentiment when his lordship and I walked together toward the court. Yes, I can see how our proximity might easily have been misunderstood."

"Misunderstood?" His eyebrows rose.

"Why, yes. What you mistook for intimacy, Mr. Newbright, was simple humanitarianism on my part. For Lord Montague claimed to be unable to make the journey unassisted.

"Of course now, in light of what you've just told

me about his womanizing, I collect that I may indeed have been gulled. But at the time, considering the force with which I'd landed, it sounded quite reasonable that he'd suffered serious injury. Oh, really, Mr. Newbright," she said peevishly, "I do wish you had made your presence known. Then you might have come to Lord Montague's aid yourself, and we'd have no need for this conversation."

Mr. Newbright let that pass. "Did his lordship describe the specific nature of his injury?" he pounced.

"Well, he did imply I'd cracked his ribs," she improvised. "And I certainly believed it possible. He's either a very good actor or he really was not feeling at all the thing. But then," she mused, "my cousin told me afterward that he thinks Lord Montague is coming down with measles. And my plummeting upon him certainly cannot be held responsible for that."

"Measles!" Mr. Newbright looked stunned.

"Yes. And at his age. Isn't it absurd," she giggled.

He laughed too, involuntarily, and she had to admit it did a great deal for his appearance.

"It does rather dim his lordship's luster. Somehow one simply cannot picture Don Juan with such an infantile disease. Still," he mused, "it could explain why he appeared rather unwell last evening."

Jemima opted for plain speaking. "You suspected he'd been shot, didn't you?"

"Why, yes," he admitted. "I did think at first that he might have been the one who snatched Jonathan West from his armed guards."

"Well, I must say that the notion strikes me as odd. I simply cannot imagine a Bond Street beau like Lord Montague exerting himself in that fashion."

"You do have a point. And it's true, as he says,

that he isn't political. Still," Mr. Newbright concluded in disgust, "I wouldn't have put it past him to do it as a lark. I'd think better of him if I could believe he'd acted from conviction."

"Whoever did do it must have been courageous," Jemima ventured.

"Or foolhardy."

"And you think his lordship belongs in the second category?"

"Neither, actually," he replied regretfully. "For it seems he could not possibly have been the one."

"Oh?" was all she could think of to say.

"No, Lady Lawford assures me that he arrived here far too early for him to have rescued Mr. West."

Eager as he was to implicate Lord Montague, Jemima was surprised that he'd accept the testimony of her addlepated aunt. She refrained, however, from saying so.

"And," he shrugged, "if he's actually suffering from measles and not a bullet wound—"

"Yes, that certainly would let him off the hook."

"No, not entirely." His face set stubbornly.

"I don't understand. Didn't you just say—"

"I know. And it may be mere prejudice on my part, but, still, I can't help but feel that Montague's somehow involved. At the very least there's the matter of the curricle. I think he must have lent his rig for the escape. After all, it's bound to be the fastest thing around."

Jemima could certainly vouch for that. Her blood boiled as she recalled her wrecked coach and splattered cloak. "Would that be a crime?" she asked.

His lip curled. "Oh, I'm sure he'd plead ignorance."

"Well, he did point out that his curricle has been often copied."

"Oh my suspicions aren't based just on that one circumstance, Miss Forbes. There's also the matter of his being here."

"Surely that's not so odd. After all, he's a friend of Marcus."

"Not so anyone would have noticed until recently. Oh, your cousin would have sold his soul to be a part of Montague's set. But, frankly, that select group is miles above his touch."

"Don't forget, though, that his lordship and Marcus are related."

"About as close as you and I to Adam," he sniffed. "No, Miss Forbes, I'm convinced that the only reason Lord Montague wheedled an invitation—and I do know that coming here was his own idea entirely—was because of Lawford Court's location. I believe that Jonathan West's rescue is not just the work of one person. I believe there's been a plot. Hatched most likely at White's Club for Gentlemen, where both Montague and Mr. West are members. I think that his lordship's part is to see to it that West is smuggled out of the country. That's why I intend to keep him under surveillance. And," he added, "that's why I felt compelled to warn you against him."

"Well, as I said, Mr. Newbright," she rose to her feet, "the warning was unnecessary. But still, I've found our conversation quite enlightening."

"Have you indeed?" He also stood. "Well then I'm most gratified." His eyes grew quite intense. "For I do value your good opinion, Miss Forbes. I don't know if you are aware of it, but your aunt and uncle are most eager for us to become acquainted."

"Well, actually I think they intended for you to meet my sister," she qualified.

"Then it was my good fortune that you came instead."

Since Jemima hardly knew which way to look, let alone how to answer such a statement, she simply bade him a hasty good day and hoped it wasn't too apparent that she'd retreated.

It wasn't until she'd reached the sanctuary of her bedchamber that Jemima realized she'd forgotten all about the library book that she'd gone to fetch.

Chapter Eleven

JEMIMA WAITED UNTIL Mr. Newbright must surely have left the library, then started back to find her reading matter. As she was passing Lord Montague's bedchamber, the door opened and he emerged. He was wearing a riding coat and top boots and, in Jemima's opinion, looked absolutely ghastly. She said so.

"Thank you very much, Miss Forbes, for those words of encouragement," he glowered as they walked together toward the stairs. Jemima glanced at a nearby maid who was watching them curiously while she dusted and lowered her voice. "Get back in bed, you idiot, before you drop."

"Mind your own business, Miss Forbes." But as he spoke he turned paler still and reached out a hand to the wall for support. "Gad, the whole place is spinning like a top," he muttered.

The maid left, reluctantly, to answer a bell. Jemima sighed and transferred his hand to her shoulder. "This is fast becoming a habit, but here, lean on me. You're going back to bed."

"The devil I am," he said between clinched teeth, while at the same time he became a dead weight that almost bore her to the floor. "I'll be all right as soon as I get some fresh air."

"Look, I'm in no mood to argue. In point of fact, my

knees are buckling. Now do I help you back, or do I call someone else to do it? I'll tell you one thing, I'm not anxious to be seen supporting you again." With great difficulty she somehow managed to get him back into his chamber, where he collapsed with a groan upon the canopied bed. "Where's your man?" she asked, looking at him anxiously. Beads of perspiration glistened on his forehead. His eyes were closed.

"Gone back to London."

"You mean he's left you?"

"He got word that his father's seriously ill."

"Fustian," she said grimly. "The truth most likely is that he didn't wish to be involved in whatever coil you've got yourself into. And I can't say as how I blame him. Now let's take off this coat."

First she removed his soft leather gloves, over his protest. "Oh, my heavens, you're burning up," she said as she felt his hands. "Let's get a look at that wound of yours."

"See here, Miss Forbes," he growled as she began to undo the silver buttons of his dark blue coat, "you're taking entirely too much upon yourself. I think perhaps you've exaggerated the importance of that kiss I gave you. Believe me, you should not."

She paused long enough to give him a withering look, which proved quite ineffectual since his eyes were closed. She was forced then to rely on the spoken word and managed to pack as much disgust into her tone as possible. "Lord Montague, if you're under the impression that you sent me away swooning from that overpracticed kiss of yours, you sadly mistake the matter. To be honest, I found the incident rather less than memorable." His dark eyes fluttered open. “And let me say further that I'm no more anxious than your absconded valet to become enmeshed in your affairs. But it doesn't seem I have much choice in the matter. Now try to raise up a bit so I can get this confounded coat off.”

He almost fainted from the effort, a state of affairs that left her quite unnerved. “Gad, you're cow-handed,” he muttered when he'd recovered a bit.

“Don't blame me, blame your tailor. The sap-skull left no maneuvering room.”

“That sap-skull is an artist. Probably the finest tailor in the world.”

“Well, I'm sure he didn't expect his artistic creation to be worn over a gun-shot wound.” She was busily unbuttoning his fine cambric shirt.

“You know, you really do seem to lack for modesty, Miss Forbes.”

Jemima was thinking something along those same lines herself as she noted with interest that his thick chest hair was black in contrast to his fair locks and that he was surprisingly muscular for such a useless member of society. But as she uncovered the clumsy bandage on his shoulder and observed the angry red streaks running out from underneath it, she quickly lost her clinical detachment. “Oh, my heavens, I think you have blood poisoning.”

“Watch it—ouch!” he protested as she gave the cloth a jerk that tore it loose. The wound immediately began to seep blood and pus.

“Oh that's—that's—horrible.” She turned green and sat down quickly on the bed.

“A real Job's comforter you turned out to be.”

“Well, that settles it. You have to have a doctor.”

Jemima started to slide down off the high bed but he clasped her wrist to detain her. The fact that the grip was little stronger than an infant's was even more upsetting.

"No, don't," he said weakly. "It's not just my own hide I'm afraid for. There's Johnny to be considered. He's depending on me."

"Well, you'll be no use to him dead, now will you? I'm getting you a doctor."

"No, dammit."

"Yes, dammit. You can ask him to say nothing. Dr. Jackson seems a very kindly man."

"He may be kindly, but he's not likely to be self-destructive. He'll not wish to be a party to a crime. Or to allow his friend Sir Walter to become implicated. Use your head, Miss Forbes."

"Well . . ." she hesitated. "But something has to be done for that wound. It's awful."

"It just needs time, that's all. I'll be better after I rest a bit. I have the constitution of a horse."

"And the brain power, too," she countered. "Oh, very well then. I'll give it a few hours. But if you're not better, then I'm sending for Dr. Jackson."

"That's all I ask. And . . . thank you. I'm in your debt, Miss Forbes."

"No, you are not, Lord Montague. For I'm not doing this for you." She slid off the bed. "I'll be checking back to discover if you're alive or dead. And, by the by, everyone, Mr. Newbright included, thinks you are coming down with measles."

"With what?" His eyes flew open.

"Measles."

"My God, how lowering. Wherever did they get a mutton-headed notion like that?"

"Never mind. But if you've any sense, you'll encourage the misconception. Now try and get some sleep."

Jemima peered out into the hallway to make sure the coast was clear before she scurried to her own bedchamber. There she paced back and forth, her conscience in a turmoil; despite its best effort, she made up her mind.

It took a while to locate Miss Jane Lawford. She finally found her in the kitchen, deep in consultation with the cook. "Could I see you a minute, please," she whispered.

Jemima wasn't sure Jane really believed that she was suffering from a painful boil. Her new friend seemed to look at her rather oddly. But when asked if she knew of a remedy that could help draw out the poison, Jane replied that she had the very thing.

Jemima followed her halting lead down into the cellar where the walls of a tiny room were lined with shelves containing medicines and herbs. "Why it's a regular apothecary's shop. Dr. Jackson wasn't teasing then when he said you were a rival."

"Oh, he likes to exaggerate," Jane smiled. "But medicine is a keen interest of mine. I used to watch my mother make our remedies before we had the services of a competent physician." She scanned the shelves. "Ah, here it is. A comfrey salve. It should prove quite efficacious for . . . your boil."

Jemima accepted the jar with thanks and turned to go. "Oh, just a minute." Miss Lawford was looking over her shelves again. She removed a bottle, then blew the dust from off it. "Here, take this too. It's laudanum. In case your boil grows really painful. It should help you sleep and allow Nature, the real healer, to do her work."

As they ascended the stairs, Jemima chattered away about this and that to prevent her hostess from asking any questions about her fictitious malady. She had an uneasy feeling that Jane suspected something, though she could think of no reason why.

But when she was at last forced to pause for breath and Jane could slip a word in edgewise, it wasn't Jemima's health she spoke of but Bess's. "I've just looked in on your maid and can assure you that she's progressing nicely."

Jemima felt a twinge of conscience for her own neglect and vowed to visit Bess the very first chance she got. Jane then left her to return to the kitchen and Jemima fairly flew upstairs. First making sure she was not observed, she slipped into Lord Montague's chamber once more.

"What the devil!" His lordship's eyes flew open and then he groaned. "Oh, you again."

"So much for a mission of mercy," Jemima snapped.

"Well how the deuce am I supposed to get better if you keep on popping in here? You promised to give me some time, remember?"

"Oh, do be quiet. Believe me, this is the last place I'd choose to be if I were rational. But I can't just let you die of blood poisoning without lifting a finger to help, now can I?"

"Well, I am touched, Miss Forbes."

"You needn't be. I'd do the same for a spaniel."

"Damn it, woman!" he swore as she again removed the bandage with a jerk.

"Oh, do be still; someone might hear you. Besides, it couldn't be that bad."

"Easy enough for you to say. Good God!" He jumped again as she began to smear salve onto the angry wound. "I really do rue the day I splattered you with mud. The Inquisition could have used your talents."

"Don't be such a baby." She dipped her fingers back into the jar and applied a second coat.

"What, in God's name, is that loathsome stuff?"

"Comfrey. Miss Lawford swears by it."

"You told Jane Lawford about me? Damn it all, you promised to say nothing. I should have known no woman could keep anything to herself."

"I don't recall promising you anything of the kind, but, no, I didn't tell Jane about you. She thinks the salve's for me."

"Oh? And what reason did you give for needing it?"

"Boils."

"Boils!" He laughed weakly. "Boils and measles. Really, Miss Forbes, aren't there any less embarrassing diseases you could invent?"

"I fail to see any humor in the situation." She poured some liquid into the glass on his bedside table and thrust it toward him. "Sorry I don't have a spoon."

"What is it?"

"Laudanum. To help you sleep."

He gulped it down, then wiped the back of his hand across his lips and shuddered. "Are you sure you're finished?" he inquired sweetly as she prepared to leave. "You could always bleed me, you know."

"Don't tempt me, Lord Montague."

"Good day, Miss Forbes."

Jemima was pleased to note that he already sounded drowsy.

Chapter Twelve

"We must send for Dr. Jackson immediately."

Though she had often read of it, Jemima had never actually seen anyone wring her hands until her aunt did so. It spoke volumes for Lady Lawford's agitation that she had not let the presence of her niece stop her from speaking her mind. Followed closely by Marcus, she had swept into the great hall where the guests were collected before dinner and interrupted an anecdote her husband was relating to his sister and Jemima.

Lady Lawford and her son were in sharp disagreement. Her ladyship appealed to Sir Walter to make the young man see reason. Lord Montague's severe case of measles required immediate medical attention.

Marcus was every bit as distraught as his mother. "Papa, you mustn't," he protested. "Monty absolutely forbade me to call in a doctor. He l-loathes quacks. He told me so."

"I should hardly term Dr. Jackson a quack," his father replied mildly.

"No, indeed," her ladyship chimed in. "That's one thing we can say, he's as competent as any London doctor. Better in fact. For I'm sure that his treatment of my staggers did me far more good than Dr. Philpot's physic ever did."

Though her son did not actually say 'the devil take your staggers', he did look it. "That aint the point, Mama, and you dashed well know it. Told you a hundred times that I gave me word not to send for a quack—a doctor—and that's that."

"But what if he should die here?" she wailed and the nearest house guests looked at their group curiously. "Then what would everyone say?"

"There, there, m'dear," Sir Walter said soothingly. "People seldom die of measles. And I'd think it a highly unlikely fate for a young man in the pink of health."

"But it does happen. And if it should happen while Lord Montague is under my roof, well, you know what the consequences of that would be. I'd be cut from society, that's what. And so would you be, Marcus." She turned to her son while Jane and Jemima exchanged quick glances, their eyes twinkling.

"Well, I will be in either case," Marcus observed glumly, "for Monty swears that if I call in a doctor, he'll cut me."

"Oh, my heavens!" Lady Lawford clutched her heart. The tall ostrich feathers that adorned her brassy hair were set aquiver. Jemima looked at her aunt with some alarm, wondering if perhaps she should run and fetch the sal volatile.

"Oh, how could his lordship say such a thing," her ladyship moaned. "He should have stopped to consider poor Marcus's feelings. Not to mention mine. Oh, Sir Walter, what shall we do?"

"Well, at the moment, my dear, we shall go in to dinner." Riggs had appeared at the dining room entrance and the guests were looking their way expectantly. "I tell you what. To set your mind at ease, Jane here can look in on his lordship directly after dinner. You don't mind, do you, Jane?" Since the question was rhetorical, he went on to reassure his wife as he offered her his arm. "You know how greatly Dr. Jackson respects our Jane's nursing skills. She can determine what's best to be done. And if in her opinion his lordship requires the services of a physician, well then we've no choice but to override his wishes in the matter. But in the meantime Riggs is glaring our way. Let's not allow the soup to cool."

During a dinner that seemed interminable and did indeed consist of three removes, Jemima hardly knew what she was eating. And when the ladies at last left the dining table for the drawing room, and Jane excused herself to go look in on the patient, her nervousness increased until it almost reached the epic proportions of her aunt's.

Jane returned just as the gentlemen rejoined the ladies, and Jemima completely lost the thread of a tedious story that an elderly widow had been telling for the last ten minutes while they shared a sofa. She watched her aunt, uncle, and cousin huddle around Miss Lawford and would have given all she owned for the ability to read lips. Still, there was no mistaking the relief that soon appeared upon her aunt Ada's face. But as for Miss Jane, well, Jemima had already learned that that lady did not give much away in her expression.

"I don't think you've heard a single word I've been saying," the old lady remarked crossly.

Jemima turned toward her guiltily. "Oh, indeed I have. You were describing your youngest child's horrendous case of measles. It must have been quite dreadful."

"My next to youngest," the dowager corrected severely. "The baby did, of course, eventually contract them." She proceeded then to describe this malady, spot by spot, until Jemima thought that she would surely scream.

Lord Montague's absence seemed to have cast a pall upon the assemblage, particularly affecting the young ladies in the group. Suggestions for dancing fell upon unreceptive ears. A few of the older guests did decide for cards. To Jemima's relief, their numbers worked out evenly and she was not required to play. The relief was short-lived, however, for Mr. Newbright singled her out and stayed by her side like sticking plaster, forestalling any chance for a private word with Jane.

A rather desperate Lady Lawford suggested that they might all enjoy some music and asked for volunteers. Daughter after reluctant daughter, prodded by apparently tone-deaf mothers, played and sang until the entire company's teeth were set on edge. It was a blessed relief when the tea tray appeared early.

It was going to be a long, long night. Jemima sighed to herself as she dismissed the maid who helped her prepare for bed. She felt she could not possibly wait till morning to discover the state of Lord Montague's health. Then she scolded herself for indulging in hypocrisy. In truth she was less concerned about his well-being than with her own involvement in it. If it should become known that she'd aided and abetted this lawbreaker, was that in itself a crime? Whether or not, it was bound to bring the roof of Lawford Court down about her head.

She was just about to climb reluctantly into bed when a soft knock came at her door. "May I come in?" Jane asked as she opened it.

"Oh, yes. Please do."

"I thought I'd best check on all my patients," she explained as she walked with Jemima toward the fire and they pulled two wing chairs closer to its blaze. She smiled at her friend's puzzled expression. "Your boils? How are they?"

"Oh, that." Jemima colored. "Can you believe I'd almost forgotten them?"

"Why, yes, I can believe it," Miss Lawford replied solemnly.

"Your salve is certainly a miracle cure. Why the moment I smeared it on I felt an instant relief." Jemima discovered she was babbling. "I know it sounds impossible, but my boil—there was only one, you see," she added in an attempt to reduce her whisker, "has completely disappeared."

"Well now that is miraculous. I can't say the comfrey's effect upon Lord Montague has been quite that dramatic, but you'll be glad to hear that his wound appears to be healing nicely. I take it that you had some real cause for concern."

"Oh, dear. You know then."

"Let's just say that I suspected. For somehow your story of needing the salve for yourself didn't quite ring true. But your agitation did, so I thought it best not to question you too closely. Then, too, I'd seen you help his lordship into the house earlier. Had his wound become putrefied?"

"Oh, yes. It looked absolutely dreadful. But he made me promise not to tell anyone else. So I felt compelled to do something on my own."

"I see. Well, let me congratulate you. You'll soon

eclipse my own medical reputation. I thought your bandage was applied quite skillfully. A pity about his lordship's neckcloth, however," she smiled.

"Not in the least. The conceited dandy must have two dozen of the things. All starched to a fare-thee-well," she added in disgust. "They were the very deuce to tie. But they did serve to hold the dressing in its place. I used a strip from his shirt for that," she explained. "It was quite soft, actually."

"So I noticed," Jane laughed. "His lordship does dress well, doesn't he? Poor Marcus is almost green with envy. I hope he never learns that you ripped up one of those lovely cambric affairs. That's possibly the most expensive wound dressing in history."

"Oh, well, as to that, I wasn't the one who destroyed the shirt. His lordship had already ripped it up to bandage himself. Not that I would have minded in the least," she added spitefully.

"You really don't approve of him, do you, Jemima?"

"I don't approve of the type, actually. Complete care-for-nothings, except for being bang-up-to-the-nines with the most exquisite tailoring, most expensive rigs. All fobs and sticks and quizzing glasses. Gaming . . . boxing . . . racing . . . all the rest. No, I just happen to think Lord Montague and his ilk are a useless lot, parasites upon society."

"Goodness,", Miss Lawford laughed. "I do think you've just described your cousin Marcus."

"No, Marcus is even worse. At least Lord Montague is the genuine article and not a copycat and a toadeater."

"Tell me, Jemima—it is all right to call you that, is it not?"

"Oh, yes, please do."

"And you must call me Jane. But what I'm curious about is this. Given your strong dislike of his lordship—or of his *type*, at any rate—how did you come to help him?"

"Well, to tell the truth," Jemima confided, "I hardly gave it any thought. I just did what seemed necessary at the time."

"I think most people would have fetched a doctor," Jane mused, "or at least have dumped the problem in my brother's lap."

"But, if I had done, Lord Montague would have been arrested. And, well, even though I may not approve of him, I would not wish to be a party to that."

"No need to sound apologetic. That's understandable."

"But that's only part of it," Jemima went on to explain in a rush. "I think I mostly did what I did for Clarissa's sake. For if Lord Montague is arrested, well, then it's bound to lead to Mr. West's discovery." She stopped abruptly. "You have, of course, realized it was Lord Montague that rescued Jonathan West?"

"Well, yes, I had figured that much out, Jemima."

"I did not mean to insult your intelligence. He, of course, denies it."

"I collect he'd have to. For if discovered, he's in a great deal of trouble.

"But I'm not sure I do understand just what Clarissa has to do with it all, though come to think on it, you did mention, I believe, that Jonathan West has published some of her poetry?"

"Yes, he did. Which pleased her enormously, of course. For I understand that the *Orpheus* publishes some of the very best—Lamb, Byron, Wordsworth, Shelley—just to name a few."

"Indeed, she is in exalted company."

"But the main thing is that she and Mr. West have been corresponding ever since. And, absurd as it sounds, I think Clarissa is in love with him."

"Oh, it does not sound in the least absurd, I assure you. Few things that involve women's emotions ever do."

"So I simply could not be a party to his capture. For I know my sister would never forgive me. But I must say," she added glumly, "I don't enjoy feeling like a criminal. Tell me, Jane, do you think that what Mr. West wrote was so very terrible?"

"It was certainly ill-advised. But, still, it's hard to view plain speaking as a criminal act. My brother believes that the Regent must regret his hasty actions in that affair. Perhaps he's somewhat relieved at the matter being settled in this fashion."

"And I suppose," Jemima mused, "that Lord Montague was rather heroic at that. One man against three armed guards, I mean to say."

"Oh he was a regular swashbuckler. No doubt at all on that score." Jane studied her new friend closely. "And I suppose it could be called heroic, depending upon one's definition of the word."

Jemima picked up on her tone. "Oh, surely," she protested, "you, too, are not going to warn me against falling in love with Lord Montague. I can assure you that there's not the slightest need."

"And I can assure you that I would not dream of doing such a thing. I'm well aware that it would be a complete waste of time."

Jemima thought it best to change the uncomfortable tack of the conversation. "The thing that bothers me most in this whole business," she said, "is my uncle. I would not for the world see him harmed by it. Do you think we should let him know that he's harboring a criminal?"

"No." Jane was most emphatic. "Walter has enough problems without this. And if it does become known, why then he is truly innocent. Which no one will dream of questioning."

"Well, let's just hope that Mr. Newbright doesn't confide any more of his suspicions to him. He believes that if he can bring Mr. West to justice, it will be the making of his political career."

"Did he actually say that?"

"Not in so many words, perhaps, but he certainly implied it."

"Well I expect he is mistaken. As I said, I'm not at all sure that Prinny would welcome any more publicity in the matter. He could be quite anxious for the business to die down. And I greatly doubt that he'd be pleased to have Lord Montague implicated. His lordship is from a powerful, and admired, family, you know. Our Regent is unpopular enough without making them his enemy. So you see, we may even be doing Mr. Newbright a service by keeping his lordship's secret. How is that for wrapping our sins in clean linen, Jemima?" She laughed as she rose, with some difficulty, to her feet.

"Well, I must confess you've made me feel better." Jemima walked with her toward the door. "If only everyone will continue to believe in the measles story." She stopped suddenly in her tracks. "He will get well, won't he?"

"No reason he should not. He's young and healthy. And he was certainly sleeping soundly when I looked in on him. He didn't even rouse when I changed the dressing."

"Oh, well, I expect that was the laudanum."

"You did give it to him then? Well that probably was a good idea. How much did you give him?"

"I'm not sure exactly. About a third of a tumbler."

"Good God!"

"Was that too much? I thought he needed sleep."

"Well, it's certainly not wonderful then that he didn't rouse. Oh he should rest splendidly, Jemima, dear. I'll not be in the least amazed if he sleeps straight through Christmas."

Chapter Thirteen

JEMIMA PASSED A restless night. And when she did sleep fitfully, it was to dream that she'd poisoned Lord Montague. "I meant it for the best," she kept explaining to a corpulent accuser who looked remarkably like the Price of Wales.

At the first hint of dawn, she abandoned the notion of sleep and threw back the covers, shivering as her feet touched the icy floor. She slipped into her dressing gown and slippers, then cautiously opened her bedchamber door. All was clear. No one was stirring. She tiptoed rapidly down the hall.

Relief was blessed. Lord Montague was breathing. Regularly and deeply. And his color, so far as she could determine underneath the stubble of beard, seemed healthy. Carefully, so as not to disturb him (though if Jane was right she could play the bagpipes in his ear), she unbuttoned his shirt and loosened the dressing. Then she almost crowed aloud. The angry streaking had subsided. The wound appeared to be healing nicely. Very gently, she applied more of the comfrey, then covered the salve with a clean dressing.

The medical part of her mission now accomplished, Jemima stood back and surveyed his lordship with an artist's detachment. Having at last captured the vision in her mind's eye, she picked up the other pot she'd brought along and set to work.

"What the devil!"

His lordship sat up suddenly and struck out with flailing hands, sending the pot flying.

"Oh, my God!" He groaned suddenly as he closed his eyes and clutched his head. "Miss Forbes," he said from between clinched teeth, "just what in the name of all that's holy are you up to?"

"Right now," came the muffled reply from beneath the bed, "I'm trying to find the blasted rouge pot. Oh, here it is." She emerged to hold it up triumphantly.

"Look, Miss Forbes," he squinted her way hostilely, "I should not have to point out the impropriety of your being in my bedchamber. I especially should not have to point it out while suffering from the champion of all headaches."

"Yes, I expect you do have the headache," she said contritely, recalling the quantity of laudanum she'd give him. "But on the whole I think you must agree it's a small price to pay for the fact that your wound is so much better."

"By Jove, it is, isn't it," he said after peering underneath the bandage. "I see you've changed the dressing. Well, thank you very much," he added grudgingly. "But now if you'll kindly remove yourself from my—just what the devil do you think you're up to?" he barked as he grabbed her hand.

"Oh, blast! Now see what you've made me do. I've smudged it."

"Have you lost your mind? Just what are you doing with that rouge pot?"

"Giving you spots, of course. You can't very well have the measles without them, now can you? Hold still a minute. Just one or two more and we'll—oh my heavens!" She froze in the act of application. "What's that?"

"Someone's coming, you ninnyhammer. Hide!"

Still clutching her pot of rouge, Jemima dived beneath the bed once more, straightening the dust ruffle behind her to insure concealment.

"Oh, it's you, Marcus," she heard Lord Montague say in a voice that had become decidedly more invalidish. "Best not come too close, old boy. Contagious, you know."

"Oh, I say," her cousin's appalled voice whispered across the room, "You've come all out in spots."

"Have I, by Jove? Oh, well then, that's all to the good."

"Is it?" Mr. Lawford sounded doubtful.

"Most definitely. It means I'm practically cured."

"It does?" The doubt mounted. "If you don't mind my saying so, Monty, it doesn't look it. Not to mince words, old fellow, you look the very devil."

"I don't doubt it," his lordship said dryly. "But I'm perfectly serious. Just as it's darkest before the dawn and all that sort of thing, measles are reddest right before going away entirely."

Beneath the bed Jemima pressed her finger under her nose to keep from sneezing.

"Well, I never heard that before." Marcus still spoke in a projected whisper. "But it does stand to reason, I expect."

"In my family at least. The Montagues are, in fact, quite noted for fighting off the measles. Once the blasted things break out, why then they're good as gone. Just like that." His lordship snapped his fingers.

"By Jove!" Marcus said admiringly, "That is remarkable."

"So there's no need to be concerned. Go on back to bed now. Decent of you to look in on me."

"Well, I've been devilishly worried. Felt responsible, actually. After all, it was my nodcock of a cousin who brought the plague here."

Jemima stiffened with indignation.

"Oh? A bit of a care-for-nothing then is she?" his lordship inquired innocently.

"You don't know the half of it. Oh, but I forgot. You do know actually. Look at the way she tongue-banged you."

"Hmmm. Yes. Regular fishwife, I'd say."

"Always has been a firebrand. Why the little hoyden shoved me in the ornamental lake when we were only six."

His lordship clucked sympathetically. "Oh, well, don't refine too much on it. We all have those unfortunate relations that we'd prefer to keep hidden away in some closet. Or underneath the bed.

"But as I was saying, don't risk infecting yourself, Marcus. I'm already feeling much more the thing. So take yourself on back to bed."

"Very well, then, I will. If you're quite sure there's nothing I can do?"

"Well there is one thing, actually. Would you mind ordering me a pot of coffee? Very strong. I seem to have the champion of all headaches. Feels as if an anvil's being pounded inside my skull."

Marcus eagerly promised to see to it immediately. As the door closed behind him, Jemima sneezed noisily.

"God bless you."

"And the devil take you, sir." She came crawling out from underneath the bed.

"A care-for-nothing fishwife, indeed," she repeated

bitterly as she dusted off her dressing gown. "That's certainly gratitude for you. And after all I've done."

"I don't recall asking for your help, Miss Forbes. Oh all right then. I'm being rag-mannered. I'll admit it. Thank you for all you've done for me. I am grateful, really. But I'll be more grateful if you'll leave me in peace now."

"Gladly." She picked up her rouge pot. "I don't suppose you'll need this anymore—given the rare recuperative powers of the Montagues. Of all the gamon!"

His lordship grinned. "I thought I was rather inventive. Deuced clever, you could even say."

She sniffed. "No, I couldn't. For no one but a complete gudgeon like my cousin would have— Oh my heavens!"

She dived once again beneath the bed where she remained throughout a seemingly interminable period of time while his lordship was served a steaming pot of coffee and a quantity of freshly baked light wigs. The heavenly aroma drifted tantalizingly beneath the bed where Jemima lay fuming with her finger pressed once again beneath her nose, listening for the door to close at last.

"Kerchoo!" She emerged once more and swiped ineffectually at her dressing gown while glaring at the rouge-dotted peer.

He was gulping down his coffee like a man who'd just crawled in from off the desert. "Couldn't you have at least waited till I was out of here to order breakfast? Of all the inconsiderate, self-indulgent—"

"Sorry I can't ask you to join me," Lord Montague grinned evilly as he slathered butter upon his roll. "Just one cup, you know. Besides, I wouldn't wish you to catch my measles. Hey, just what do you think you're doing?"

Miss Forbes had helped herself to one of the light wigs from his plate and was popping a huge bite into her mouth as she crossed the room.

"Oh, I say." She paused by the door and addressed him thickly. "Would you please tell the chambermaid to dust beneath that bed? She's been shirking her duties disgracefully. I'd see to it myself, your lordship, but it might be misconstrued."

As usual Jemima opened the door a cautious crack; then seeing no one in the hallway, she ran on tiptoe back to the sanctuary of her room.

Chapter Fourteen

JEMIMA HAD CRAWLED in bed again merely to get warm, but she fell asleep immediately. As a consequence, she overslept and found quite an assembly gathered in the dining chamber when she went in to breakfast.

"Ah, Jemima," her uncle teased, as she filled her plate and took a seat beside him, "I understand you've been a slug-abed this morning. No walk? No horseback ride? I certainly hope that doesn't mean you're sickening for something. I'll not believe it. You look absolutely blooming, my dear."

"And speaking of the sick," Marcus informed the company in general through a mouthful of pound cake, "I'm happy to report that Lord Mon—Monty, I mean to say—is greatly improved. It would not surprise me in the least," he beamed, "if he rejoins us today."

This bit of news perked up the company no end, Jemima noted. The ladies in particular seemed to come to life.

Mr. Newbright appeared rather less ecstatic. "Well then, he can't have had the measles," he pronounced.

"Oh, he definitely had them," Marcus countered. "I grant you, measles don't seem at all the sort of thing he would have." There was a tinge of disappointment in his voice, as from one who has just noted feet of clay. "But when I looked in on him early this morning, he was spotted as anything. Measles. No doubt about it."

"Then he won't be joining us."

"Oh, but that's the remarkable thing about it. Monty assures me that once a member of his family blossoms, well, the disease has run its course. He says he could be cured at any moment."

"Sounds pretty farfetched to me," Mr. Newbright sniffed. "If measles play favorites and defer to the peerage, I never heard of it. Are you quite sure that's what he has?"

"Of course I'm sure. His face looked as if it'd been tamboured all over with little red dots." Jemima choked a bit on her roast beef and required a very large drink of water. "I don't know why you keep wanting to question the thing, Newbright," Marcus said crossly. "If you don't believe me you can ask Maggie our chambermaid. She said she was half afraid to hand him his coffee for fear she'd catch 'em."

"Well, now, I am sorry for it if I struck terror into her heart," a lazy voice drawled from the doorway.

All eyes turned toward Lord Montague. Though he did look rather interestingly pale, and though the lines around his eyes still bespoke the headache, he most certainly did not look like a sufferer with measles. In fact, he dazzled. He was wearing a maroon superfine coat with sterling buttons, topped by a snowy cravat tied in the waterfall; his dove-colored pantaloons hugged his muscular thighs and calves, then disappeared into gleaming Hessians adorned with silver tassles.

"There, what did I tell you?" Marcus shot a triumphant look at Mr. Newbright.

That gentleman eyed the viscount with ill-disguised suspicion. "Marcus was just telling us of your miraculous recovery, Lord Montague."

"Oh, nothing miraculous about it," his lordship replied airily as he liberally piled his plate with ham. "Measles seem to take our family that way. We go around for days feeling like the very devil, then we blossom forth, and, presto, it's all over. My sister, as I recall, had only three spots in toto. Fortuitous considering it was the eve of her come-out."

Here Jemima giggled suddenly, and all eyes turned toward her. "That most certainly was . . . fortuitous," she managed to observe with a near-straight face.

"Oh, Lord Montague." One bold schoolroom miss leaned across the table while her friend beside her turned pink with embarrassment. "We were just scolding Sir Walter because there's no mistletoe anywhere in the house. And Christmas isn't Christmas without mistletoe, now is it?"

Since she and her friend followed this question with a serious bout of giggles, Lord Montague did not feel called upon to answer. He merely smiled.

The schoolgirl, however, found this ample support. Others around the table began to tease their host about his oversight. "Must be getting up in years, Sir Walter, to have forgot to order mistletoe." An ancient gentleman winked broadly at the company. "Thank God, I can still remember what it's good for."

This brought on gales of laughter while Sir Walter held up his hands in mock defense. "Well now," he said, "I grant you it's a grievous oversight. Particularly from someone like me who prides himself on keeping alive the old customs."

"And that's the best custom of the lot," the elderly gentleman cackled, and his audience joined in dutifully once again.

"But I can only conclude sadly," Sir Walter went on to explain, "that if there's none in the house, it means that the gardeners couldn't find any."

"We always used to get up expeditions and go for it ourselves," Marcus told the gathering. "Remember, Papa? The prime spot for mistletoe was the wood around Baldwin Manor."

"Oh, do let's go!" The schoolgirl clapped her hands, and the other young people at the table joined in her pleading.

"We cannot trespass on private land," their host said repressively.

"Oh, is there a law against mistletoe poaching?" The self-appointed wit collapsed with laughter. Once more the company obligingly chimed in.

Sir Walter was adamant, however, that the mistletoe expedition should confine itself to the Lawford lands.

"Oh, very well," his son agreed. "But I do think we should look in that direction."

"You will come, will you not, Lord Montague?" Miss Lydia Evans, a pretty young lady who had been the object of Marcus's attention during the entirety of her visit, dimpled coquettishly.

Marcus intervened before his lordship could reply. "I don't think that would be such a good idea, actually. It's quite a tramp. Wouldn't want you to have a relapse, old man."

"Of course," Sir Walter offered, "it would be possible to drive quite near the wood. Then perhaps the walk would not be strenuous. That is if you think you'd like an outing, Lord Montague."

"Oh, do say you'll come," Miss Evans pleaded. "And do drive your curricle. Mr. Lawford here assures me that it is all the crack. I can't tell you how I long to ride in it."

The breakfasters looked a trifle shocked at this blatant hint, but his lordship merely smiled politely. "Then indeed you must certainly do so. But you will have to wait your turn since Miss Forbes has also been longing to try out my rig, and I've promised to give her a spin at the first opportunity. It would seem that your time has arrived, Miss Forbes."

Once more Jemima choked. She was now the object of her fellow diner's stares, which ran the gamut from shocked to outraged. As soon as she'd recovered sufficiently, she opened her mouth to decline the privilege. She was stopped, however, by a look from Lord Montague. From a lesser mortal, it might have been considered pleading.

Thirty minutes later Jemima stood with an obviously miffed Miss Evans in front of the main entrance to Lawford Court and watched with a jaundiced eye as a black and red curricle drawn by two matched grays swept round the circular carriage drive and came to a halt beside her.

"Do you think you might manage to look admiring?" Lord Montague inquired beneath his breath as he climbed down to help her in just as Marcus, driving a slightly less dazzling rig, pulled in behind him.

"I don't see why I should," she answered crossly, but in a similar undertone. "If it's admiration you're after, why don't you take Miss Evans?"

"And cut out my good friend Marcus?" His eyebrows rose. "What kind of cad do you take me for, Miss Forbes?"

"I don't think you really want me to answer that. Tell me," she asked as he gave his whip a crack and sprang his horses, "is that what you told my cousin, that you gave poor Miss Evans a set down for his sake?"

"I don't consider that I gave Miss Evans a set down. But to answer your question, yes, I did let Marcus know that I'm aware he's developed a tendre for the young lady. Otherwise, I'd have been delighted to have her company myself."

"And he believed that?"

"Of course. Why ever not?"

"Well then he's an even bigger gudgeon than I thought."

They were soon sweeping out of the main gate and onto the highway, where he increased his speed and she clutched her bonnet. "Now then, do you mind saying why you singled me out for this honor?"

The eyes he cut toward her were wide with innocence. "Why, you did ask to ride in my rig, didn't you?"

"You know perfectly well that I didn't."

"You're sure? Now that's odd, for I do seem to recall that on our very first meeting you talked at length on the subject of my equipage. Are you quite certain that you didn't ask me then to take you out for a spin?"

The look she gave him was speaking.

"Oh, well then, my mistake. But it's a natural one. It is the more usual thing with young ladies. It simply didn't occur that you might prove an exception."

"You aren't going to tell me why you brought me along, now are you?"

"I think it was because I mistakenly believed you wouldn't ask so many questions." He glanced back across his shoulder as they approached a curve. "All right then, hang on, Miss Forbes."

"What are you doing?" she gasped as his lordship's whip snaked over the backs of his team with a fearsome crack.

"Outrunning Marcus," he grinned.

"Oh, my heavens, are you stark raving mad?"

She had previously thought their pace excessive. Nothing had prepared her for this new burst of speed. She released her bonnet to allow it to fend for itself while she clung with both hands to her armrest. The bonnet was immediately swept off her head. It flew like a kite, tugging at her neck with its ribbons.

"You id-idiot slow d-down!" Her teeth rattled. "Are you t-trying to kill us?"

Behind them, faintly, she could hear Marcus shouting. His lordship appeared deaf to either cousin.

"Slow down, you fool! You can't do that with just one good arm!" Jemima recognized his intent to turn off the highway.

"Oh no? Just watch me."

Then, with no noticeable reduction of its speed, the curricle swung precariously upon two wheels and headed toward two crumbling pillars. Jemima closed her eyes and prayed.

Chapter Fifteen

"YOU CAN OPEN them now," her companion chuckled. Jemima did so and discovered that the rig had righted itself and passed successfully between the gate posts, and that they were traveling up a weed-choked lane.

"I was right the first time, wasn't I?" she remarked conversationally. "You really should be banned by law from driving. There's something about the act of picking up a pair of reins that turns you from a reasonable human being into a mindless menace."

"A reasonable human being? Well now, coming from you, Miss Forbes, that's high praise indeed."

"Don't try to pretend you missed my point," she said crossly as they rounded a bend in the driveway and he did slow down his grays. "By the by, you do realize that you're trespassing?"

"How else was I to get rid of Marcus? Besides, this is where the mistletoe is, isn't it?"

"Yes, and I expect that's not all that's here either." She gazed around her at Baldwin Park where weeds and undergrowth ran riot over what, in previous generations, must have been an attempt at order. "What are you doing?"

"We'll walk from here," he replied, guiding his

team off the carriage road into a small grove of trees and bushes.

"Been here before then, have you?" she inquired as he picked up a napkin-covered basket, then helped her down from their hidden rig.

"Don't ask so many questions. Now let's see. The woods Marcus described should be in that direction." Montague took off cross-country with Jemima doing her best to keep up with him.

"Hold it! I'm caught here!"

"Oh, for God's sake." He looked back impatiently. She was struggling with a pair of blackberry tenacles that were caught in her pelisse. "You might look where you're going, you know," he grumbled as he set down his basket and carefully worked the briars loose from the kerseymere.

"How could I? I was too busy looking where *you* were going. For I daren't take my eyes off you. I forgot to bring along a pocket full of bread crumbs, you see, to scatter for a trail back to your curricle."

"You really are the one for dramatizing a situation, aren't you? Damn!" He pulled off a glove and sucked at his pricked and bleeding thumb. "Come on. It shouldn't be much farther now."

They set out once again with Lord Montague leading the way through the undergrowth. He did stop occasionally to pull low-hanging limbs out of her pathway or help her over a fallen tree or muddy ditch, and on one of these occasions she remarked, "At first I was concerned with losing sight of you and having to find my own way out of this wilderness. Now I'm more concerned over having to drag you out."

"Don't be. I'm perfectly fine."

"That's a stupid comment from a man who was at death's door only yesterday."

"I've already remarked on your talent for exaggeration, haven't I? I was certainly not at death's door. I merely had a fairly superficial wound that became aggravated when I removed the bullet." He turned rather green at the recollection. "It did get a bit infected, but now it's healing nicely, thank you. Of course if it makes you feel like some sort of heroine to believe you saved me from dying, well, so be it. Come on." He started off again, with no noticeable reduction of his pace.

"Ingrate!" she muttered to herself as she set out after him.

Jemima was soon watching her route even more carefully. Once again blackberry bushes had taken over the terrain. "Remind me to come back here with a pail next summer," she remarked to the world at large, then almost ran into his lordship. He had come to a sudden halt behind a massive oak and was peering round it across what once must have been an expanse of lawn but was now rampant with weeds and bushes. Beyond it, upon a slight rise, stood a decaying manor house, saved from complete collapse, or so it appeared, by the thick growth of ivy that held its stones together. Its chimney stacks were crumbling. Its window-panes were either cracked or else missing entirely. A Corinthian column in a once-imposing portico had fallen, to be replaced by a rough-hewn wooden prop.

"They say it's haunted," Jemima whispered.

"I can well believe it."

"Would you like to see inside?" They both jumped,

then spun around when a third voice spoke behind them.

"Oh, Mr. Baldwin." Jemima clutched her heart. "You startled me."

The ex-convict, still wearing his fisherman garb, stood regarding them pleasantly. An ancient flint-lock gun rested comfortably on his shoulder. "I am sorry," he apologized. "I fear I did creep up on you. I heard noises and rather expected to find gypsies." He paused expectantly.

"Oh." Not quite knowing what else to do, Jemima took refuge in her best drawing room manners. "Mr. Baldwin, may I present Lord Montague? He's staying at Lawford Court. Mr. Baldwin, your lordship, is the owner of the hall there."

"I've heard of you, of course," Mr. Baldwin said after the two men had acknowledged the introduction. "You won a curricle race to Brighton a few years back. Unfortunately," he smiled ruefully, "I had put my blunt on some other cove."

"Then you couldn't have heard *much* about Lord Montague." Jemima did not sound admiring.

"No, actually I hadn't. You must have just come down from Oxford then. Now, of course, your reputation both as a boxer and a bruising rider has become the stuff of legends."

Up until this point Jemima had considered Mr. Baldwin a sensible man. But now he seemed as prone as Marcus to fan the flames of his lordship's conceit. "You really must forgive us our trespasses." She put a stop to the flattery. "It seems our nonesuch here has got us lost."

"Oh, indeed?"

"Yes, we left his famous curricle—or its successor,

anyhow—a few miles back. We're looking for mistletoe and have lost our bearings it would seem."

"That, Miss Forbes, is an out-and-out whisker." Lord Montague ignored her glare. "The truth, Mr. Baldwin, is that we're *flagrant* intruders. We heard that the most likely place to find mistletoe is on your property."

"That's quite true and you're certainly welcome to it," Mr. Baldwin smiled. "But I'm afraid you're nowhere close. Come on. I'll take you there."

As Mr. Baldwin led them away, Jemima noticed that his lordship studied the crumbling manor house covertly. But his face revealed none of the turmoil that she suspected was going on inside.

They walked on for another mile, with Jemima longing for the pair of stout boots that were tucked away in her wardrobe at home while the two men chatted easily about London life. She kept waiting for Montague to make some kind of gaffe that would embarrass the recent resident of debtor's prison, but fortunately the conversation stayed clear of such troubled waters. "Oh, here we are," Mr. Baldwin cut short an account of his one and only meeting with Beau Brummell to exclaim. "Behold—mistletoe!" They stood on the edge of a thick wood, where indeed in the tiptop branches of the most towerlike trees, green bunches of the parasite could be seen.

The Christmas greenery was not the only thing that they discovered. Mr. Lawford and Miss Evans were tramping toward them across an open field from the opposite direction. They were both glaring indignantly.

"Where the devil did you get to?" Marcus demanded when they came within speaking range.

Jemima would have bet a monkey that this was the first time he'd failed to fawn on the viscount. She liked him better for it.

"We wondered if you were deliberately trying to get away from us." Miss Evans sounded equally aggrieved.

"Oh, not a bit of it," Lord Montague assured them with a perfectly straight face. "Miss Forbes here kept urging me to show off my gray's paces, and then I'm afraid I took a wrong turn onto Mr. Baldwin's property. Oh, Mr. Baldwin," he turned politely to their guide who had been standing a bit apart, "may I present Miss Evans and Mr. Lawford?"

Miss Evans murmured "How do you do," while at the same time Marcus looked even more thunderous. "We know each other," he said sulkily.

"Your servant, ma'am." Mr. Baldwin bowed Miss Evan's way, then turned to coolly appraise her escort. "Well, I see you've become a man, Marcus, while I was . . . otherwise occupied. Beg pardon. I should, I collect, say 'Mr. Lawford.' "

"Come on." Marcus rudely ignored Mr. Baldwin's civility and jerked his thumb to indicate the way they'd come. "We are trespassing, you know. Thought me father made it quite clear we shouldn't come here."

"I'm afraid my curricle is in the other direction, old man," Montague said placatingly. "Got totally turned around. But just name the spot, and we'll meet you."

"Well, now, since you are here," Mr. Baldwin said pleasantly, "it seems rather absurd, wouldn't you agree, to leave without your mistletoe. I can assure you, *Mr.* Lawford, that it is not contaminated. No need to advertise where it came from. Oh, by the by, may I inquire just how you planned to go about getting it down?"

"Well," his lordship grinned suddenly, "in my case I'd intended to send Miss Forbes shinnying up the tree after it. She's a perfect wizard when it comes to climbing trees. Did you know that about your cousin, Marcus? Of course she still has a few kinks to work out in her descent technique. But practice makes perfect, Miss Forbes." He gestured to the nearest mile-high oak where the mistletoe hung tantalizingly in the top branches.

"Your sense of humor also has a few kinks that require work, your lordship."

"Well, if you've no objection, please allow me." Mr. Baldwin put the stock of his gun to his shoulder and took careful aim. There was a deafening explosion, and then a ball of dislodged greenery came tumbling down through the bare branches. "Oh, well done!" Jemima cheered as she ran to retrieve it.

Mr. Baldwin repeated the procedure several times and soon, despite those clumps that had become hopelessly lodged in the tree limbs, the party had gathered an impressive pile of mistletoe. But since they'd made no more provision for carrying the greenery than for getting it down, a spirited discussion followed. Marcus took strong exception to his cousin's suggestion that they make a hammock of his lavender greatcoat and pile the collection on it. But then when even Miss Evans pointed out that since the mistletoe was perfectly clean and their rig only a short distance away, he should neither freeze nor despoil his finery, he reluctantly gave in.

"Oh, by the by, Mr. Lawford," Mr. Baldwin asked as the group was coming to a parting of the ways, "has your bailiff mentioned anything about gypsies in these parts?"

"Why no. Have you seen any?"

"Not *seen*, no. But someone broke into my house yesterday. No, let me amend that. There was no need to break in actually. It's never locked. But whoever it was cleaned me out of food. And since we've never been plagued with that sort of theft in these parts—the natives may help themselves to game and fowl on the foot or wing, but never roasted," he explained to the newcomers—"I expect it's gypsies. You might warn your bailiff to keep an eye out."

Marcus thanked him rather stiffly for the information. Jemima thanked him most profusely for the mistletoe, and the party went its separate ways.

"Well, it looks as if you lugged those provisions for nothing," Jemima remarked a bit later on when his lordship deposited the heavy basket he'd been carrying back in the curricle.

"The crowd we collected did spoil my plans for a private picnic."

"Fustian. You didn't bring all that food for us. Why not admit it?"

"I admit nothing." He skillfully guided his team out of the thicket.

Jemima refused to let the subject drop. "Well, at least you know your friend isn't starving," she remarked a bit later as they traveled down the highway at a more sedate speed than she'd dreamed him capable of. "But then of course he's likely to be arrested for theft at any moment."

"Again, what a Job's comforter you turned out to be. Not that I've the slightest notion of what you're talking about, of course."

"Oh, rubbish. I don't see why you even try to keep

up this silly charade. Ever since Mr. Newbright told of his rescue I've known that you're the one who freed Mr. West. I knew that you were bleeding, and I also knew that you'd had plenty of time to do it, never mind the impression you tried to create that you arrived at the court as early as your baggage."

"My, aren't you the clever one. Bow Street would love you."

"I'm not trying to be clever. Clever doesn't even come into it. I saw what I saw. The point I'm trying to make is that there *isn't* any point in your keeping up such a pea-brained pretense."

"The point could be, my dear Miss Forbes, that I'm trying to keep you out of this thing."

"Well it's a bit late for that. The only real point is, what do you plan to do now?"

"How the devil should I know? Maybe if I had a moment's quiet to think, I could figure out something."

"Well, surely you must have had some plan of action."

"My plan of action was to get Jonathan to France. And I thought that a deserted, haunted estate was the ideal place to leave him temporarily while I made arrangements. But I didn't count on being shot, or on having the ubiquitous Mr. Newbright on my heels, and most especially," he ended bitterly, "I did not count on having the deserted estate suddenly become occupied. By the by, while we're on that subject, how do you happen to be acquainted with Mr. Baldwin?"

Jemima went on to explain that he had driven her to the court after the coach wreck. "Then I met him again when I was riding on the beach, and he was working on his boat."

She could almost see his ears prick up. "What sort of boat?"

"How should I know. I'm no expert. A fishing boat, most likely."

"Well, you surely know if it's large or small."

"No need to snap my head off. Isn't that purely relative? It's certainly not the size of a Channel packet. Nor is it a punt."

"Oh, come on now. You can do better than that. Is it simply a rowboat or are there sails?"

"Sails. Definitely sails."

There was a minute's pause. "What's your impression of Mr. Baldwin?"

"If you mean do I think he's the type who'd jump at the chance to smuggle Mr. West into France, frankly, I doubt it."

"Oh? The risk wouldn't have to be all that great, and I'd pay handsomely. He certainly appears to need the blunt."

"Money's your answer for everything, isn't it?" she glared.

"No, not entirely. But it does smooth out a lot of the rough places. Tell me, why don't you think it would work with Mr. Baldwin?"

"Because he's just come from prison, and unless I miss my guess, no power on earth could make him risk returning there."

"My God!" He looked genuinely shocked. "So that's why Marcus was so insufferably rude to the man."

Jemima let that pass. She was not inclined to tell him that there might be a more compelling reason.

"Do you happen to know what his crime was?"

"Failure to pay his debts. His family has been addicted to gambling for generations, so he said."

"He told you that? You seem to have become bosom friends in record time."

"Mr. Baldwin felt it only fair to warn me about his reputation. After all, he wasn't to know that I'm accustomed to consorting with criminals."

"Touché!" Montague lapsed once again into silence, a faraway look in his eyes. Jemima broke the spell as they entered Lawford Park. "Tell me," she asked, "what is Mr. West like?"

"Jonathan?" He seemed to have some difficulty adjusting to the here and now. "What's he like? Well, I'll tell you this much, Miss Forbes," he replied with a weary resignation, "he's about the last man in England who'd be capable of borrowing a beached fishing boat and sailing himself to France."

Chapter Sixteen

THE LOOK THAT Lady Lawford bent upon her niece was not cordial. She was stretched out upon a Grecian couch, still wearing a dressing gown, and had just put aside a copy of *Ladies' Magazine* to devote her full attention to the scold that she intended to deliver.

"I am shocked, Jemima. No, to put it even stronger, I am mortified. Humiliated. To think that a niece of mine should behave in such a brass-faced manner. Throwing yourself at Lord Montague's head like some . . . some . . . lightskirt! You may rest assured, young miss, that I intend writing your mother a full account of your wanton behavior."

Jemima reined in her temper. "Well, aunt, if you really intend to write Mama that I'm throwing myself at Lord Montague's head, I'll simply have to tell her that you much mistake the matter."

"Oh, there's no mistake. Miss Evans was kind enough to inform me that you had, as bold as brass, invited yourself to ride in Lord Montague's curricle."

"Well, now," Jemima's eyes glinted dangerously, "that was indeed kind of Miss Evans. And did she also inform you that she herself had asked for the same privilege?"

Her ladyship looked slightly taken aback. "No, but even if such a thing did happen, which I'm much inclined to doubt, the two cases would not be at all the same."

"Oh? And why not, pray tell?"

"Because, miss, in the first place it's common knowledge that Marcus and Miss Evans have an understanding. Lord Montague would never have misconstrued her request as anything but a genuine interest in his famous rig."

"But I could not have a similar interest?"

"Also," Lady Lawford continued, ignoring the interruption, "Miss Evans is a young lady with an established social position and immense fortune. Even if she did display an interest in Lord Montague himself, which I do not for one moment believe, you may be sure that he would treat her with the utmost respect. Whereas in your case . . . well, not to put too fine a point upon it, the only thing you might expect from a gentleman of the first stare is a slip on the shoulder."

"You are offensive, madam."

"Just as well if my plain speaking offends. It's time you learned what's what. And I'm not through speaking my mind, young lady." She raised her voice and her body as Jemima turned to leave. "There's one more thing I'm compelled to say about your shocking behavior this morning. Miss Evans tells me that you actually entered the Baldwin estate after your uncle had expressly forbidden it."

"Surely you can't blame me for that, aunt. Hadn't you better send for his lordship and read him the riot act?"

"Don't be impertinent. You could certainly have prevented it."

"How, pray tell? You've already pointed out that Lord Montague can only hold me in contempt."

Her aunt ignored this bit of logic and moved on to other sore points. "There is also the matter of Mr. Newbright to be considered."

"Indeed? Well, pardon me if I fail to see what Mr. Newbright has to say in the matter."

"A great deal. For it would not be at all wonderful to find that you've sunk yourself beneath his contempt. And after all your uncle has done to promote a match between you."

"Between him and Clarissa, surely."

"Between him and one of my widowed sister's daughters! And the least we might expect is your gratitude. For Mr. Newbright is a prime catch for you. His political prospects are excellent. And though he is not possessed of a fortune, well, Sir Walter would not like me to say so, but he is prepared, under favorable circumstances, to provide my nieces with a *small* dowry. So you'd best watch how you go on, Jemima. It would not do for society to form a disgust for you. Be warned."

"I am, Aunt Ada. Now is there anything else you wish to say?"

"Yes, as a matter of fact. Miss Evans has also told me that you seem to be on quite easy terms with Mr. Baldwin. Well, it will not do. Our family is not on speaking terms with that—that—*reprobate*, and I'll thank you to keep that fact in mind while you're under this roof. Very well, you may go now." She waved her hand dismissively and picked up her magazine again.

As she left the chamber, Jemima's eyes were so blurred with angry tears that she blundered right into Miss Jane Lawford. "Oh, I am sorry," she mumbled and would have hurried on, but Jane put out a hand to stop her. "Please, may I have a word?" she whispered, indicating with a nod at her sister-in-law's closed door that she didn't wish to make her presence known.

What Jemima longed for most was a chance to be alone and give vent to her rage, but good manners overrode this course of action. "Certainly," she whispered back.

"You'll have to excuse me, though," she added a bit later in a normal voice once her chamber door had closed behind them. "I've just gone through a most unpleasant interview with my aunt, and I fear it's left me in the foulest temper imaginable."

"I know." Jane limped over to the dressing table stool and sat upon it, while Jemima crawled up on the bed and leaned back against the headrest. "I'm sorry to add to your distress by saying that I overheard at least part of the conversation. The truth is," she smiled rather painfully, "just as I'd prepared to knock I happened to overhear Mr. Baldwin's name. Then after that I fear I listened shamelessly. Is it true, then, Jemima, that you've made his acquaintance?"

"Why, yes." Jemima went on to tell her then about her three encounters with Mr. Baldwin.

"So you know that he's been in prison?" Jemima nodded. "Tell me, how does he seem?"

"Well, you do realize I've no basis for comparison. And I've never seen him dressed like a gentleman. So I really don't know what to say," she floundered, "except that I quite liked him."

Jane smiled her painful smile again. "I'm very

glad to hear it. I had hoped prison life had not changed him overly much. It's bound to have taken its toll, of course."

"Then you're not bitter?" Jemima blurted before she'd taken time to think. "I should not have asked that," she reddened.

"I see then that you've heard the story of my elopement."

"In part. I just assumed that Mr. Baldwin was the man involved. I am right, am I not?"

"Yes, and it's natural enough that you should wonder about my feelings in the matter. So, to answer your question, no, I'm not the least bit bitter. Unlike my brother, I did not find it wonderful that a gentleman would be interested merely in my fortune."

She quickly cut off the protest forming on Jemima's lips, making it quite plain that the subject was closed. "But this is not the only reason I wished to speak to you. I have some Christmas baskets to deliver and had wondered if you'd like to go along. But since you've been out all the morning, perhaps you'd prefer to rest."

Resting was the last thing Jemima desired. After the unpleasantness with her aunt, she thought a breath of fresh air might be the very thing and said so. They soon set out in a well-loaded gig.

Miss Jane proved to be a more than competent driver, guiding her horse skillfully up the narrow and sometimes crooked lanes that led to the tenant houses that they visited. Jemima went in with her each time, helping to carry the heavy baskets. She was struck in every case by her new friend's cordial reception. Her aunt might nominally be the lady of the manor, but the reality was obvious. Jane's genuine concern for the sick and elderly had earned her first place in the tenants' hearts.

"Would you like to drive along the beach?" Jane asked when they'd delivered the next-to-last basket to a cottage that lay within the sound of the surf. "I love to look at the wintertime sea. But then, of course," she laughed, "I also love to look at the spring, summer and falltime sea."

Jemima assured her that she would like it above all things. When they finally reached the flat stretch of pebble and sand by a precipitous route that had her clutching the edge of her seat and closing her eyes, she was not overly surprised to see Jane turning her horse in the direction of the Baldwin estate.

Miss Lawford seemed to pick up on what she was thinking. "I thought we'd leave a basket for Mr. Baldwin," she remarked, a bit too casually. "A sort of welcome-home present. That is, if you don't mind delivering it. The hall is no distance at all from the beach. In fact, we'll be able to see it quite plainly."

Jemima had it on the tip of her tongue to explain that Mr. Baldwin was not living in the hall when she suddenly thought better of it. Someone was living there who had a greater need of Christmas charity than Mr. Baldwin. And if Jane's basket could prevent his having to risk exposure by venturing forth to look for food, that was all to the good.

Still, she felt guilty about deceiving her new friend and was weighing the greater good against the lesser evil when fate took such ethical considerations out of her hands. She felt Jane grow tense and followed her gaze on down the beach.

This time she had no problem recognizing Mr. Baldwin, even with his back turned. He was wearing the same old clothes and appeared to be mending his sails. At the sound of the gig's approach he stood up and turned their way.

Jemima watched Jane from beneath her eyelids as they drew near the boat. She had gone rather pale, but the hands holding the reins were quite steady as was her voice once she'd pulled her horse to a halt beside the beached fishing craft. "Hello, Edward," she said. "It's nice to see you again."

Jemima might as well have not been present. Mr. Baldwin never took his eyes from Miss Lawford's face as he walked slowly toward the rig. "And you Jane? How have you kept? Still, there's no need to ask. You're even more lovely than before."

Jane laughed at that, spontaneously, looking, so Jemima thought, the girl she would have been when he ran off with her. "Oh, Edward," she said with a catch in her voice, "thank God prison hasn't changed you. You're as free with your Spanish coin as ever."

"Spanish coin? I think not, Jane." He spoke quite seriously, his gaze intense. "I'm not proud of all the things I did back then, but I do recall I always told you the truth about yourself."

"I believe you've already met my friend, Miss Forbes." Jane's need to change the subject was blatantly apparent. Mr. Baldwin shifted his gray eyes from her face and smiled his charming smile. "Why, yes. We met again only this morning. As you can see, I kept a souvenir." He gestured to a sprig of mistletoe stuck into a buttonhole of the short coat he wore.

"I'm glad to see you had some reward for all your efforts," Jemima smiled back, then went on to explain to Jane that he'd shot down the greenery for them.

"You've lost none of your skill then. Mr. Baldwin, Jemima, was the nemesis of all the local rabbits. Are you settling in well, Edward? I hope things have not been too . . . awkward for you."

"Not at all. Oh, I'll grant you that our neighbors haven't come calling, leaving their cards. But after my sojourn in the Fleet, I can assure you I find solitude bearable. Not that I've been all that alone. Not only did I have our adventure this morning and now this encounter, just a bit ago another visitor from Lawford Court came by on horseback and stopped to chat. A Mr. Newbright. Most polite fellow. Quite intense. And full of questions."

"Whatever about?" Jane asked, while Jemima tried to look no more than politely curious.

"Seemed to be interested in gypsies. Evidently Marcus mentioned that I'd had some food taken. He wondered if I'd actually seen any strangers about. Seemed rather disappointed that I hadn't. I think he was hinting that I give him a tour of the hall. Seems he's heard rumors of our ghost and is quite interested in that sort of thing, though I will say he hardly looks the type. But if that's really what he wanted, I'm afraid I didn't pick up on it. I felt the need to get my boat seaworthy while the good weather holds. Besides," he smiled, "it would have been a waste of both our times. No self-respecting ghost goes wandering in broad daylight."

"It is a fascinating place." Jemima gazed at the crumbling edifice that towered above the cliff. "I wouldn't want to meet your ghost, but would you mind if I took a closer look at your house? That is, if you're not in a hurry, Jane."

It must be obvious that I'm trying to give them some time alone, she thought as she climbed down from the rig. But neither seemed inclined to resist her clumsy tactic. "Oh, shall I take the basket out of the dampness?" she asked. "I can leave it on your portico, Mr. Baldwin."

"Basket?" he inquired.

"It's just a few things from our kitchen," Jane explained. "Christmas pudding and the like."

"Oh, have I made your charity list then? Widows, orphans, ex-convicts."

She looked distressed. "I did not mean you to think . . . It was supposed to be a welcome home gift."

He reached out and took her hand. "Please don't look like that. I was merely funning. I can see my joke was in poor taste, however."

Jemima looked from one to the other then lifted the basket out of the gig and trudged off with it.

As far as she could tell, neither party was aware of her departure.

Chapter Seventeen

JEMIMA WAS HUFFING and puffing after her climb up the steep cliff path. It was a relief to set the basket down upon frost-blighted grass and survey the manor house. As her eyes traveled over the all-filthy, often-cracked, and sometimes-broken windows, she hoped that there was someone up there looking down. Even so, the thought caused her to shiver. The notion of unseen eyes, even those of Mr. Jonathan West, following her was creepy.

She forced herself to stare even harder at the windows, squinting her eyes, letting them travel systematically over the entire face of the old building. It kept its secret. No flicker of movement was discernible. Still, all that dirt afforded sufficient concealment. Pity there were no curtains to betray a presence by their movement. Not that it was necessary. For by now, though she could not have explained just why, she was convinced that she was under observation.

But what exactly was Mr. West to make of a young lady trespassing on the Baldwin estate, carrying a basket? Her first thought was to yell his name. But she immediately realized that such a course was foolish. He'd no way of knowing that she had his best interests at heart. He was probably going to ground in the attics or the cellars at this very moment. Besides, Mr. Baldwin might come along and hear her.

And there was a second problem. Though her mission was to see that Mr. West got the food intended for Mr. Baldwin, she now realized that she couldn't just put the basket down and trust him to come and take it. For even if he did not actually come face-to-face with Mr. Baldwin, that gentleman, when he failed to find his Christmas basket, would most probably conclude that his "gypsies" were camped inside the house. He was bound to send for the authorities.

As she wrestled with the problem, Jemima absentmindedly rubbed her aching arm. Jane must have packed enough provisions in that basket to last the winter. Of course! That was it. Mr. Baldwin had certainly not inventoried the contents of his Christmas gift. So he'd never know if most of it was missing. She'd make a bundle for Mr. West in the covering napkin and put it inside the house. But first she'd try to let him know what she was up to, in hopes that he was watching.

Jemima moved to within full view of all the windows, carrying the basket. She then waved it back and forth like a signal lantern before she set it down. Next, she removed the napkin and flapped it in the air a bit, shaking off imaginary crumbs. Well, if Mr. West did not realize by now that she'd brought him food, he could not possibly have the superior intellect with which he was credited. But just to make doubly sure— She tucked the napkin into the collar of her pelisse then peered into the basket. Chicken, ham, beef, cheese, all sorts of cakes and a Christmas pudding. She helped herself to a ginger nut. Then, feeling ridiculously like a character in the pantomime, she carried it to her mouth in an exaggerated arc.

"Miss Forbes, what are you doing?"

Her shriek was muffled by her mouthful.

"Really, Mr. Newbright," she accused, after she'd swallowed the ginger nut amid some choking. "You should not creep up on a person in that manner."

"I was not creeping up." He emerged through a clump of rhododendron. "I was here before you."

"Then why didn't you make your presence known instead of scaring me out of my wits?"

"Because frankly, Miss Forbes, I was curious about your strange behavior."

"Strange behavior? I don't know what you mean, I'm sure. Oh, if you're referring to the fact that I helped myself from the Christmas basket, I'll admit to feeling rather sharp set after my climb, and, well, perhaps I should not have done so, but Miss Lawford does tend to play Lady Bountiful, and there's enough here for an army, let alone one man. So I hardly think it will be missed." She tried to look shamefaced.

"And for whom is the Christmas basket intended, Miss Forbes?"

"Why for Mr. Baldwin, naturally. I've been helping Miss Lawford make her deliveries, and since she's unable to climb the cliff, I brought this one myself. And," she added, hoping to further cloud the issue, "I certainly intended to tell her that I helped myself to a ginger nut."

"Hmm. It seems rather odd to me—not to say entirely inappropriate—that Miss Jane should include Mr. Baldwin in her charities."

"I don't consider it odd in the least. It's the season of good will, you know. Mr. Baldwin is my uncle's closest neighbor, and from the looks of his property, he could use a bit of charity."

"I don't think even Sir Walter's Christmas spirit would extend to Mr. Baldwin. And I doubt he knows of his sister's . . . generosity."

"Then I'll not mention it," Jemima said pointedly. "By the by, Mr. Newbright," she went on the attack, "you have not said why you happen to be skulking about."

"Skulking? I can assure you I was doing no such thing."

"Well, you certainly crept up on me."

"I did not creep. I told you before, I was simply standing here."

"Behind a bush?"

They had traded roles. He was now the one on the defensive. "I was merely curious to see Baldwin Hall, that's all. It has historic significance, you know. It's quite the oldest pile in these parts, so I've been told."

"It's old all right. No doubt about that." Jemima surveyed the house with disapproval. "But I'd hardly call it a showplace. Of course it is reputed to be haunted, which gives it a certain fascination. But frankly, Mr. Newbright, I'm surprised that that sort of thing appeals to you."

"Oh, I'm not concerned with the supernatural. If it's haunted, well there has to be a rational explanation."

"Gypsies? Mr. Baldwin did mention this morning—we met him, you see, when we were looking for mistletoe—that there were gypsies in the neighborhood."

"I beg pardon, but I believe that Mr. Baldwin merely *wondered* if there were gypsies in the neighborhood."

"Oh, is that what he said? I must have misunderstood then. Fancy your being so well informed when you weren't even there."

"As it happens, I took pains to question Marcus rather closely. Frankly I find it a bit curious that your party wound up on Baldwin land when Sir Walter had expressly forbidden you to go there."

"Oh, well now, that was quite by accident." She picked up the basket and with Mr. Newbright dogging her footsteps walked over to set it and herself down on the hall's crumbling marble steps. "Lord Montague was showing off his team's paces and took a wrong turning. That's all there was to that."

"A remarkable coincidence," he sneered as he stood over her.

"Not so remarkable since we're both strangers to the neighborhood. I'm sure there was no intent," she added virtuously, "to go against my uncle's wishes."

"Not by you, perhaps."

She ignored the implication. "And though I would not for the world wish to disobey my uncle, there was no harm done surely. We gathered a prodigious amount of mistletoe, and with Mr. Baldwin's permission as it happened. So all's well that ends well, you might say."

"No, Miss Forbes, I would not say anything of the kind. For, trust me, nothing has ended."

"I'm sure I don't know what you mean."

"Do you not, Miss Forbes? You can't have forgot that I warned you once to stay clear of Lord Montague."

"Well, that's a bit difficult, you must admit, considering we are both my uncle's guests."

"So are a lot of other people. But you—alone—rode with him in his curricle this morning."

"Surely no one can take exception to that." Her protest rang a little false as she recalled the people who had already done so. "This is 1817, after all."

"Let me say it once again." He sounded like a weary tutor with a slow pupil. "Lord Montague would never take a *proper* interest in a female of your station."

"And let me tell you, sir, that I was hardly expecting him to go down on one knee to me. When it comes to that, it's the last thing in the world I would desire."

"And I feel it my duty to warn you that it's an altogether different sort of proposal you might expect from his lordship."

"Well, now you have, Mr. Newbright. But you'd have done better to save your breath to cool your porridge. Oh, I don't doubt that his lordship is every bit the rake you say he is. But I do doubt that he'd try and seduce Sir Walter's niece while enjoying that gentleman's hospitality. That would call for an even blacker character than the one you paint. Besides," she added thoughtfully, with only the slightest trace of pique, "I don't think Lord Montague has any interest of that kind in me. After the opera dancers and other exotics he's been accustomed to, I expect I must seem like an antidote."

"I quite doubt that."

"Goodness, Mr. Newbright," she twinkled up at him, "I hardly know if I've been complimented or insulted."

"Neither. You've been *warned*, Miss Forbes."

"Repeatedly, Mr. Newbright."

"Then heed it. Do not allow his lordship to use you for a cat's paw." He looked pointedly at the basket.

"You are entirely too cryptic, sir. For I don't see how he could possibly do so. The notion is, in fact, ludicrous."

"Is it?" His eyebrows rose. "Well, I hope you're right. But that would rather depend, would it not," he said softly, "upon who the recipient of that basket is supposed to be."

"I told you that," she said crossly. "Pray pay attention. It's for Mr. Baldwin. And now, if you'll excuse me." She rose and crossed the flagstones to ply the tarnished knocker, wondering what effect the hollow sound might be having on Mr. West, if he indeed was still inside.

"Mr. Baldwin is not at home," Mr. Newbright volunteered.

Oh good, she said to herself. He doesn't know that Mr. Baldwin isn't actually living here. Aloud, she asked, "Well why didn't you tell me that before I battered the door down?"

She tried the door then, expecting it to be locked. But it swung open on creaking hinges. "In that case I'll just set the basket inside. He's sure to see it when he returns."

She suited the action to the word, then reclosed the door with a reverberating slam. "Well, I really must be going, Mr. Newbright," she said politely. "By now Miss Lawford must be wondering what's become of me. Would you care to ride back with us? I'm sure we can squeeze three persons into the gig."

"No, thank you. I came on horseback."

"Indeed?" She looked about her pointedly. "And where is the animal?"

He reddened just a bit. "I left it tethered back in there." He gestured toward the wood.

"My, you really are furtive. Well, then, I shall see you shortly back at the court. Unless you intend to tour the haunted house after I'm gone, that is."

"Of course not," he said stiffly. "I'd hardly enter while Mr. Baldwin's away."

Why, he's afraid, it suddenly dawned on her. But then, she added charitably, perhaps he has every right to be. Mr. West could be a desperate man.

"I think I will wait here a bit, though, and have a word with Mr. Baldwin when he comes back. And that way," he added pointedly, "I can be certain that Miss Jane's Christmas bounty falls into the proper hands. Good day, Miss Forbes."

Her mind in a whirl, Jemima hurried back down the cliff path, hardly aware of the precarious footing. There was no doubt about it, Mr. Newbright was convinced that Jonathan West had gone to earth inside Baldwin Hall. She must let Lord Montague know of this right away. Though heaven alone knew what he could do about it. Leave for France immediately himself?

In her preoccupation, she remained oblivious of Miss Jane Lawford and Mr. Baldwin until she had almost reached the gig. She looked up then and saw them seated there together, deep in earnest conversation. And the odd thing was, they seemed even less aware of the world around them than she herself had been.

Chapter Eighteen

THE MISTLETOE WAS livening up the house party considerably. The young people had taken it upon themselves to distribute it, and there was not a doorway or chandelier under which one could stand without paying the consequences.

Jemima made this discovery when she entered the great hall before dinner. She stood in the doorway and scanned the crowd, searching for Lord Montague. She had just spied him, the center of a fawning group dominated by her aunt, when she was clasped firmly around the waist and bussed enthusiastically upon the cheek.

"Caught you, Miss Forbes!" the octogenarian crowed, amid the delighted laughter and applause of those near by.

In spite of the urgent need to speak to Montague, Jemima was diverted by the old man's enterprise. Time and again he planted himself strategically by the doorway, leaning heavily upon his cane, his weak eyes glinting lasciviously. There he would pounce upon every unwary female who entered, bringing forth gales of merriment from those well situated to observe his sport.

The old gentleman's enthusiasm soon became contagious. Other males in the assembly turned into predators, preying upon the unwary—or aware—females who happened to stray beneath the mistletoe. Jemima watched with fascination as Miss Evans casually moved "by chance" under a clump of greenery. There was no mistaking the lady's look of disappointment when Marcus, not Lord Montague, seized the moment.

Jemima was suddenly struck with an idea. Miss Evans need not be the only female to cast out lures. How better to achieve an assignation? Thereupon she strolled nonchalantly across the room, seemingly in search of someone. Once she'd come within earshot of his lordship, she added strength to this deception by inquiring in a rather carrying voice whether anyone had seen Miss Jane Lawford. Having received the expected negative reply, Jemima then continued her perambulations, to arrive, quite unawares of course, underneath the same hanging invitation that Miss Evans had just abandoned.

But unlike Miss Evans, she did not intend to leave the situation up to chance. There was no problem in catching Lord Montague's attention. He was watching her with puzzled fascination. When Jemima shot him a speaking look, he gave the briefest of nods to show that he'd understood her maneuver.

Even so, she sighed with relief as she saw him start to move her way. The sigh almost converted into a frustrated groan, however, when she was seized, for the second time that evening, about the waist and soundly kissed—this time upon the other cheek.

"Really, Mr. Newbright," she fumed.

"Really, Miss Forbes," he smirked and pointed upward to the mistletoe.

She all but stamped her foot as she saw Lord Montague stroll on by to join a group around her uncle.

"I've been wishing to speak to you, Jemima." Mr. Newbright recaptured her attention. "You don't mind my making free with your first name, do you?"

She did, actually, but thought it more politic not to say so and merely smiled.

"And you must call me Lloyd."

"Lloyd? Oh, are you perhaps part Welsh then?"

"Yes, as a matter of fact. But I do wish you would not change the subject."

"Was I doing that? I thought I was merely making conversation. I was not even aware that a subject had been introduced."

"I am trying to tell you something quite important," he said impatiently. "Oh bother!" Riggs had just appeared to announce their dinner.

As Jemima watched Lord Montague give her aunt his arm, the faint hope died that he might somehow find a way to sit beside her. Mr. Newbright, on the other hand, stuck to her like glue.

After the vicar, who had joined them for the evening meal, had asked a lengthy blessing, Jemima turned politely to her dinner partner. "I believe you wished to tell me something, Lloyd."

"Not here," he said beneath his breath, while he helped himself liberally to a dish of collops. "This is not a subject one should introduce in public."

Oh my goodness, Jemima panicked, he can't be about to offer for me. She knew he'd do almost anything to curry Sir Walter's favor. But surely not to the point of proposing matrimony upon such a brief acquaintance. And if he did so, what would her answer be?

She was painfully aware of her duty to her family. Her mother was saddled with five impecunious daughters to be settled. And it certainly did not help the situation that the eldest, a hopeless dreamer, had fallen in love with a fugitive from justice. But Mr. Newbright—Lloyd! She was not at all certain she liked him, let alone— Her agitation was not soothed by the discovery that Lord Montague was watching her from his place above the salt.

The meal went on forever. As Christmas approached, the Lawford's modestly situated friends and poor relations were beginning to lose their awe of their surroundings. Even the presence of a member of the nobility now failed to dampen their holiday spirits. And the alacrity with which the several footmen jumped to refill the rapidly emptying wine glasses did nothing to stem the rising tide of merriment.

This jollity was brought on in the main by the same old gentleman who had been so busily employed beneath the mistletoe. He seemed to be the family clown and kept the group in stitches with his anecdotes. These, as the meal progressed, grew more and more risque. One particular story, having to do with a fresh-faced curate and an old-maid member of his choir, so sent a young schoolgirl into the whoops that she wound up with an acute case of hiccoughs. This caused the company to laugh even harder, with the exception of the young lady's mother who frowned a warning at her daughter across the table.

The signal for the ladies to retire came at last. But then Jemima had to endure another long wait in the drawing room. She was developing the headache from sheer anxiety and debated whether or not to use it as an excuse to flee to the sanctuary of her room.

Still, if she did so, it would merely postpone the

moment. And, frankly, she did not feel that she could endure the suspense much longer. At last, with doomed resignation she watched the largely inebriated gentlemen file into the room.

But Mr. Newbright was not among the company. Nor was Lord Montague. Jemima was trying to sort out that ominous circumstance when the two at length returned together. Both gentleman's eyes immediately sought her out, but it was Mr. Newbright who, after a curt nod to his companion, came striding toward her across the room.

He sat beside her on the settee and whispered, "I'm sorry to have kept you waiting, but I needed to keep an eye on a certain individual. But perhaps there's still time to say what I wish to say before Lady Lawford organizes us for the evening's entertainment."

"You wish to speak to me here?" Jemima asked nervously.

"Why, yes. No one's paying us the slightest attention. And it would look rather odd if we left the room together don't you agree?"

"I suppose so." She stole a glance at him. He was bursting with the desire to speak. His eyes fairly danced with suppressed excitement.

"I wanted you to be the first to hear," he whispered.

"Well, yes, I collect I should be first. Since Mama isn't available."

"What the devil—err, deuce, I mean—does your mother have to do with the matter? What I have to say is for your ears alone. For the moment at any rate. But once this evening's drama has played itself out, well, then everyone will know about it."

"I see," she said, then realized that she didn't see

in the least. "Mr. Newbright, what on earth are you talking about?"

"*Lloyd*, please."

"Well, Lloyd, then. But I do wish you'd come to the point before my aunt presses us into the quadrille or whatever."

"Very well. But before I do so, I must say, Jemima, that I owe you the deepest apology for ever suspecting—though only vaguely suspecting, you understand—that you could be in any way involved in the Jonathan West affair. My reason for this ever-so-slight suspicion, you see, was that I've had ample opportunity to observe what fools females tend to make of themselves over Lord Montague. And so, I feared he might be using you to do his dirty work."

"So you said." She tried to look offended instead of guilty. "And just what caused you to change your mind?"

"Why the fact the Mr. Baldwin told me that Miss Jane had prepared a Christmas basket for him, which you were entrusted to deliver. And I must confess that up until that point, I had entertained a *slight* suspicion that your food was meant for someone else."

"Surely you can't believe that I have a soft spot for gypsies?"

"Of course not," he said impatiently. "As I've just regretted, I did imagine—for an instant—that Lord Montague had gulled you into carrying provisions for Mr. Jonathan West who is, I'm convinced, holed up inside Baldwin Hall."

"Oh, really?" Jemima somehow managed to get the words out, even though her throat had suddenly constricted. "Why on earth would you think that?

Wouldn't he have headed straight for Dover to cross the Channel?"

"I think not. I think his rescuer realized that the authorities would be watching every ship that sailed. I think the intent was to hide Mr. West away until the hue and cry died down, then book passage." He was obviously pleased with his deductive powers.

"But surely not at Baldwin Hall? You can't be thinking that Mr. Baldwin is in any way involved."

"N-no," he admitted with some reluctance. "While Edward Baldwin's character is certainly suspect, I don't believe he knows anything about this business. You see, I questioned him a bit, quite subtly, and I really don't think he's even heard of Jonathan West, let alone been a party to that gentleman's escape.

"You have to remember, Jemima, that Mr. Baldwin has just been released from prison. And no one in these parts seemed apprised of his release before it happened." He paused significantly. "What I'm saying is," he continued when she offered no reaction, "that as far as anyone knew, the Baldwin estate would be deserted at this time. What better place to hide a wanted felon?"

"But who in London would have known that?" she objected.

"Lord Montague for one," he said.

"But I thought you'd finally concluded he could not possibly be involved—oh, for all sorts of reasons you named."

"He's involved all right." Newbright's eyes took on a fanatical light. "I don't know just how. But I think now that the witnesses became confused in all of the danger and excitement. I'm now convinced that the guard who fired mistook his target and it was Mr. West, not his rescuer, who was shot. Or it could be that the man missed entirely and simply made up the tale to save a bit of face.

"But the truth will be known soon enough," he gloated. "For our quarry's now at bay. What I had wished to tell you was that I've spoken to the local magistrate and he's organized a party to search Baldwin Hall tonight. In fact," his eyes sought out the ormolu clock that held pride of place upon the nearer mantle, "the raid should be taking place right now at this very minute."

Chapter Nineteen

"OH, MY HEAVENS!" Jemima choked.

It was fortunate for her composure that her aunt Ada came swooping down upon them just then in order to consult Mr. Newbright concerning the rules of a hotly contested game of snapdragon, which some of the young people were playing.

Jemima quickly murmured her excuses and hurried across the room, hoping for a private word with Lord Montague while Mr. Newbright was preoccupied. But much to her disgust his lordship was accosted by the two giggling schoolroom misses. She stood by impatiently, all but tapping her foot, till at last she caught his eye.

But even then he took forever to become disattached. And his stroll toward her was so nonchalant as to make her long to scream. "Well, you certainly took your time," she hissed when he came near enough to hear her. "I need to talk to you. It's most—"

Her words were abruptly cut off as she was pulled close against him and her lips were smothered with his own.

Later on, it would occur to her that it was probably a great pity that so much expertise had to go to waste. This was her second experience of a Montague kiss, and she had not the slightest doubt that, along with his other talents, he was a nonpareil in that exercise as well. For indeed, both times, and under the most unfavorable circumstances imaginable, she had found the experience quite unsettling. And she did not for a moment question that given better times and places the kisses could have been most pleasant . . . perhaps exhilarating. But now, in this unfortunate milieu, she had little enough difficulty (save for the lengthy interval it took to collect herself) in giving his chest a decisive shove. She came out of the embrace sputtering and indignant. "Have you entirely lost your mind?"

For reply he pointed upward. She almost spit. She had not realized she'd been waiting underneath the chandelier, which in addition to its myriad prisms, fairly dripped with mistletoe. All around them, people were tittering.

"Oh, blast!"

His eyebrows rose. "A strange reaction, Miss Forbes, considering you've been trying to lure me underneath that stuff all evening."

"I've been trying to have a private word with you all evening, by hook or crook," she whispered, trying to keep a straight face for benefit of the curious. "But now there's no time to waste with this sort of foolishness. Mr. Newbright has sent the authorities to search Baldwin Hall."

"Good God! I'll have to get out of here and warn Jonathan," he whispered back.

"It's too late for that. The search is taking place this very minute. What you'd best do is take to your heels while there's still time."

"Now that would be damned stupid."

"And waiting to be arrested is intelligent?"

"It won't come to that. Jonathan won't implicate me. You can rest assured of that. And Newbright has only his suspicions to go on. No one will take his word over mine."

Jemima thought that over. "No, I don't suppose they will," she said slowly. "Which doesn't seem at all fair, I don't mind saying."

"It isn't, I'll grant you. Nor is it fair for Jonathan West to go to prison for speaking his mind. But that's the way of the world, Miss Forbes. Of course," he studied her intently, "you could always even the score by turning me in yourself."

"You know I'll not do that."

"Well, no, actually, given your egalitarian views, I wasn't too sure. By the by, do you mind saying just why you won't inform on me?" He gazed at her intently.

She wanted to hurl, *Not for the reasons you're thinking,* right back into his teeth, but the words seemed stuck in her throat. Maybe she was, after all, just one more of the hen-witted females, like Miss Evans, for instance, who'd been moved to make cakes of themselves over a handsome profile and an ancient title. "I don't like the idea of sending *anyone* to prison," she substituted lamely.

Further conversation was made impossible. Her aunt, busily sorting people out for various entertainments, swooped down upon them. Lord Montague excused himself from dancing. He had not yet recovered sufficiently, he said, for such strenuous exercise. He chose instead to join the round table of cards that was being formed. Jemima was assigned to the pianoforte to play for the dancers. On the whole she preferred her role to his. Still, perhaps cards would keep his mind off what was happening on the next estate, though she tended to doubt it.

She wanted to scream when Mr. Newbright came to stand beside her and offered to turn the pages. But he was far too keyed up to do it properly. Between looking at the clock and keeping his ear cocked for the sound of horsemen, he kept flipping pages at entirely the wrong times, causing the music to falter and the dancers to trip. "Really, Mr. Newbright, Lloyd," Jemima finally protested. "Just let me do it." After that he confined himself to sitting on a nearby chair, absently tapping his foot in time to the music, with his eyes glued on the drawing room door.

But it was not until the tea board had been produced, its contents devoured, and the company were bidding one another good night that the expected interruption finally happened. The butler entered, followed closely by a Goliath of a man wearing riding clothes, whose puffy cheeks and bulbous nose were a bright cherry red from the cold.

"Why, Mr. Carter!" Sir Walter did not try to hide his surprise. "What brings you out so late? Here, stand by the fire, man. You look frozen. Riggs, fetch a brandy."

"Excuse the intrusion, sir." The newcomer spread his huge hands close to the blaze. "Fact is, your man there asked me to wait in the hall. But since I wished a word with two of your guests, I thought this would be quicker, and we could all get on to our beds. God knows I need to."

Jemima was glad to see that everyone else appeared as curious about the untimely visit as she was. The "good nights" were forgotten, as they all pressed near to hear what Mr. Carter had come to say. Such enlightenment was delayed, however, while that gentleman took an enormous mouthful of his brandy, savored it, swallowed, smacked his lips, then immediately followed it up with another.

"You were saying, sir?" Sir Walter prodded.

"That I wished a word with your secretary and Lord . . . Lord Montague, is it?" Sir Walter nodded, and Mr. Carter looked pleased at his feat of memory. "And," he looked around him, obviously relishing his position as the center of attention, "any other company that might shed some light on this havy-cavy business. Because I don't mind saying, sir, I've no notion what to make of it. For the fact of the matter is, a lot of good men who would have preferred to be home with their families this evening were coaxed out on a wild goose chase." He directed a reproachful look at Mr. Newbright whose eager face then suddenly drained of color.

Jemima was struggling to keep her own expression under control. She tried to avoid looking at Lord Montague, but when, in spite of herself, she did so, she was awed by his composure. He was lounging against the mantle, gazing at Mr. Carter with mild interest. As Jemima watched, he smothered a yawn.

"What do you mean, 'wild goose chase'?" Mr. Newbright blurted.

"Why, I mean, sir, that we searched Baldwin Hall from attic to cellar twice over, then once again, just for good measure, and never saw a single sign of your fugitive. That's the wild goose chase to which I referred."

"Searched Baldwin Hall!" Sir Walter looked stunned. Beside him, his sister had turned deathly pale. "Why would you do such a thing?"

"Ask him." Mr. Carter jerked a thumb toward Mr.

Newbright. "The fact is, your secretary here was positive that a Mr. Jonathan West, escaped felon, was hiding out there. But now I'm forced to ask just why he was so sure."

"He was there! I know it!" Newbright sputtered. All eyes were fixed upon him. "He had to be. It's the only possible place Montague could have hid him."

"Oh, I say!"

"Mr. Newbright!"

"Lloyd!"

"How dare you!"

"He can't mean it!"

So many people, including her uncle, aunt, and cousin, spoke at once, that Jemima could make no sense at all of the bedlam. She was able to distinguish his lordship's dry chuckle, though.

Mr. Carter turned his way. "Just what do you have to say to that, sir? You are Lord Montague, I take it."

Could you even doubt it? his lordship's expression seemed to imply. But then, before he could speak, Mr. Marcus Lawford erupted. "Now look here, Carter, you've no right to—"

"Of course he has, Marcus," his lordship interrupted in a soothing tone. He then turned politely back to the Magistrate. "Am I to understand, sir, that Mr. Newbright here," he nodded contemptuously toward the secretary, "has tried to involve me in Jonathan West's disappearance? Well, I've known, of course, that he's had this bee in his bonnet for some time. But I didn't think he'd carry his daft suspicions to such extremes. You see, Mr. Carter, the bases for his accusations, as far as I can determine, are that Mr. West and I were schoolmates and that I'm very happy indeed if he has escaped. As for the latter, I think the majority of Englishmen will be of the same opinion, for I can hardly conceive of a more unjust conviction."

"Well, I'll not argue with that, sir, though in my position I collect I should." The magistrate turned then to look sternly at Mr. Newbright. "Is this indeed all you had to go on, sir?"

"No, it isn't!" Mr. Newbright thundered, his face suffused with anger. "His curricle was seen in the neighborhood where West was taken. And he may claim he had the measles, but I happen to believe that he was shot."

By this time everyone was looking at Mr. Newbright rather oddly, Mr. Carter most of all. "Measles or a gunshot wound, eh? Well I'd say that most folk would be able to tell the two apart."

While some of the company tittered at the magistrate's dry wit, Marcus claimed the floor. He was quivering with indignation. "I don't know why Newbright here is bent on vilifying Monty, but he's been at it ever since he came, and I for one am sick and tired of it. The truth is, Carter, that whereas his lordship *wouldn't* have done such a shocking thing as to take a prisoner at gun point, the fact is he *couldn't* have done so, for he was on his way here, though I can see no need to refute the ravings of a jumped-up, underbred secretary who's jealous as anything—"

"That will do, Marcus," Sir Walter interposed sternly, then turned to the magistrate. "I'm truly sorry, sir, that your evening has been wasted in this manner. Especially since the responsibility lies at my own door. Pray convey my apologies to your men. And now, unless you've any further questions, I'll not detain you longer from your bed."

Riggs ushered Mr. Carter out amid a buzz of shocked exchanges among the Christmas guests. These mutterings were accompanied by the stolen glances at Mr. Newbright who appeared close to apoplexy. As she reluctantly joined the bedtime exodus that had begun, Jemima studiously avoided looking at his lordship. But then, like everybody else, she turned to stare when Mr. Newbright wheeled on the lounging viscount.

"You needn't think for a minute that the thing's finished, Montague!" He was close to shrieking. "No, not by a long shot. For I'm on to you. And you'll not be able to lift one finger to help West escape, for I'll be watching you like a hawk every minute. You may depend on it!"

"My God, the fellow's dicked in the nob," the octogenarian loudly observed in what he possibly thought was a whispered aside. "Why the man's a regular bedlamite if I ever saw one."

Chapter Twenty

As Jemima left the room she saw Sir Walter draw his secretary aside and request a word with him. Anxious to seize the opportunity for a private talk with Lord Montague while Mr. Newbright was thus engaged, she lurked in her bedchamber, leaving the door cracked just enough to peep through unobserved. "Hist!" she whispered as she spied him in the hall. She opened the door wider and practically dragged him inside. "We need to talk."

"Not as much as I need to get out of here while Newbright's occupied," he replied impatiently. "I've got to find Jonathan. God knows what he's going through."

"Don't be a widgeon. How do you expect to find him out there in the pitch dark? There's not a sliver of moon, you know. And you can't exactly flash a lantern around and shout for him."

"Look, I don't need your sarcasm. I have to do what I—"

He was interrupted by a peremptory knock. Before either one could react the door had opened. Miss Jane Lawford limped inside. "I thought I'd find you both in here," she said.

Her face was dead white and she was obviously in the grip of some strong emotion. It took Jemima a moment to identify it as anger, so foreign was that condition to Miss Lawford's usual nature.

"How could you, sir!" She directed her wrath upon Lord Montague.

Though he did not actually reply "et tu Brute," his look implied it. "How could I what, ma'am? Surely you don't take Newbright seriously?"

"Pray don't fence with me." Her voice shook. "I'm not concerned with the right or wrong of your rescue of Mr. West. But hiding him on the Baldwin estate! Involving Edward Baldwin! That was despicable! If you yourself are discovered, with all your family's influence, you're bound to get off lightly. But a man straight out of prison?" Her eyes filled with tears. "They're certain to put him away for life, at the very least."

"Oh God!" Montague ran his fingers through his hair, playing havoc with its modish Brutus style. "Look, let's all sit down and try to discuss this rationally. You're right, Miss Forbes, there isn't anything I can do tonight. And bolt the door, will you. We don't wish to be joined by Newbright. That really would cap off a ghastly evening.

"Please believe me, Miss Lawford," he continued when they'd settled by the fire, "I certainly never intended to involve Mr. Baldwin—or anyone else for that matter—in this business. Newbright's right, of course. I'm here because Marcus happened to mention the empty estate that marched next to his. Its haunted manor house sounded ideal for a temporary hiding place. Believe me, it was a shock to learn that the owner was back in residence. One of several shocks," he added bitterly. "The first was an unscheduled bullet in my arm."

"Well it seems to me," there was a note of censure

in Jemima's voice, "that you might have expected that sort of thing when you took on three armed guards."

"The devil a bit I did. What kind of fool do you take me for? God knows I'd forked over more than enough blunt to insure that they fired over my head."

"You mean you bribed the guards?" Jemima was shocked.

"Naturally. Sorry to disillusion you. But I'm no hero."

"Aren't we rather straying from the point here?" The necessity for keeping their voices down didn't rob Jane's of its acidity.

"You're right, of course. What I was going on to say was that I'll have to contrive somehow to get out of here in the morning without Newbright seeing me. If I can't just walk out in the usual manner, well, there's always the window."

"A sheer drop of three stories?" Jemima scoffed. "Remember, you're no hero."

"She's right, you know," Jane seconded. "Oh not about the heroics. But your arm isn't nearly well enough for a rope descent, or whatever you had in mind. Besides, if you go out the window and are caught, it would be as good as an admission of your guilt."

"So you stay here and I'll go try and locate Mr. West as soon as it gets daylight."

"No, Jemima. You're not exactly above suspicion yourself. I can't allow you to get into serious trouble. I feel rotten enough about involving Baldwin."

"That's it, of course! We can't be thinking. Mr. Newbright will follow *you*. So while you lead him off on some wild goose chase in the morning, I'll be free to hunt for Mr. West on Baldwin lands."

"*We'll* be free," Jane said quietly. "It would look odd to others besides Mr. Newbright if you were gone for any length of time by yourself. But if we're delivering Christmas baskets together, no one will give us a second thought." Jane managed a weak smile. "This will possibly prove the best Christmas our tenants ever had."

Next morning the two young ladies had the satisfaction of seeing Mr. Newbright leave the dining room immediately after Lord Montague had excused himself. They waited a bit longer, then hurried to an upstairs window that commanded a view of the stable path. Their vigil was shortly rewarded by the sight of his lordship hurrying down it, throwing an occasional furtive glance back over his shoulder.

"He mustn't overdo it," Jemima commented. "He's no more an actor than he is a hero."

Jane nodded and pointed to where the secretary was skulking along from bush to bush. "It may take quite a bit of acting ability on Lord Montague's part to pretend he's unaware that he's being followed." The two held on to each other in a fit of nervous laughter.

They had decided to take the beach route again. "You'll have to be the legs, of course," Jane said. "Try to find Edward and tell him I need to see him. Carry a basket with you in case some of Mr. Carter's men have come back for a daylight look. You can say it's for Mr. Baldwin. I trust they'll not know we brought him one just yesterday."

As it turned out, there was no need for subterfuge. They found Mr. Baldwin on the beach again, working on his boat. He straightened up at their approach and regarded them quizzically as the gig pulled to a stop beside him. "More charity, ladies? Or have you joined the hue and cry after the fugitive?"

"In a way," Jane supplied. "Have you seen him, Edward?"

He came over to rest his hands lightly upon the gig shaft and look up at her. "Now do you really expect me to answer that, Jane Lawford?" he said softly. "Don't you imagine that I'd feel a bit of sympathy for some poor devil that's being hounded into prison?"

"That's exactly what I have imagined, Edward Baldwin. And I'm here to say that I don't give a—tinker's damn—about Mr. West. It's you I'm concerned with. And I'll not have you involved in this. You've suffered enough already. This is no concern of yours."

He raised his hands in mock amazement. "By George, I think you really mean it. I've never heard you swear, Jane. I wouldn't have believed you could do it."

"Don't make jokes, Edward." Tears were forming in Miss Lawford's eyes.

"Look," Jemima interposed. "You have it wrong, Mr. Baldwin, if you think we're here to turn in Mr. West. We want to help him."

"*You* want to help him," Miss Lawford corrected through her tears.

Disillusionment seemed to be running rampant. Jemima had always considered Jane a tower of strength. "Have you seen Jonathan West, Mr. Baldwin?" she asked bluntly while her friend tried to collect herself.

"Yes, as a matter of fact. After meeting you and then talking to your friend Newbright yesterday, I put two and two together. I concluded that all that food wasn't actually intended for me and that my 'gypsy' was something else entirely. So after everyone had left I searched the manor myself and discovered your Mr. West hiding in my attics.

"And a good thing I did, too. For I convinced him the house was likely to be searched by the authorities, which of course proved to be the case."

"And where is he now?"

"I think it best that you remain ignorant of his whereabouts, Miss Forbes," he answered firmly. "But he's safe enough and little worse for wear, thanks to all that food and some old blankets."

"You just couldn't stay uninvolved, now could you?" Jane's tone was bitter.

"No, I couldn't. It hardly seemed possible. It's not as if Mr. West's one of your criminal types. And God knows I'm something of an authority when it comes to those. Why, would you believe it, the poor cove doesn't even owe anyone money," he grinned.

"It's no funning matter."

"Perhaps not. Then to give a straight answer, no I couldn't throw him to the wolves. Any more than you could with your tender heart, Jane."

She held her head up and looked him straight in the eye. "But that's just what I will do, Edward Baldwin, before I allow you to risk going back to prison on his account."

"Have no fear on that score. I've no yearning myself to repeat the experience."

"Don't try to pull the wool over my eyes, Edward," she snapped. "I saw the supplies in your boat when we first drove up. You're planning to take that wretch across the Channel."

"Now couldn't I just be planning a fishing trip?"

"I know what you're up to, and I will not allow it."

He sighed. "Come now, Jane, be reasonable. Even if the wretch, as you call him, were capable of sailing this thing himself," he nodded toward his craft, "which, believe me, he is not, I couldn't just donate my boat, now could I? Fishing's become an important part of my livelihood."

"I meant what I said. I'll suggest to the authorities that they'd do well to keep a sharp eye on your boat."

"That's hard, Jane. God knows I appreciate your concern. But actually the risk is minimal. After last night the authorities are convinced that West's nowhere within miles of here."

"Stop it!" Jemima jumped in before Jane could form her rebuttal. "This is getting us nowhere. Jane's right, Mr. Baldwin. You should not be involved. You're right when you say that Mr. West's no sailor. But Lord Montague is. Or at any rate claims to be," she amended, recalling his "heroics." "We all agree that Mr. West is his lordship's responsibility. So it seems to me that he should simply 'borrow' your boat, unbeknownst to you, of course, and then return it. And it wouldn't hurt," she continued to think aloud, "if you went to stay with friends while all this is going on. Then, if anything does go wrong," she shivered, "you won't be involved."

"Thank you for your concern, but an ex-convict has no friends."

"And how can Lord Montague manage an escape with Mr. Newbright following him every minute?" Jane threw in dampeningly.

"By the by," Mr. Baldwin asked, "where is Montague at the moment? Needless to say, Mr. West is anxious to contact him."

The ladies went on to explain that his lordship

was decoying Newbright as far away as possible while they tried to discover what had happened to Mr. West. Jemima broke off in the act of describing Mr. Newbright's tactics to strike her forehead. "Of course!" she exclaimed. "That's it! The very thing! Why did I not think of it earlier?"

"What are you up to now?" Jane looked uneasy.

"Why the solution's so obvious that we were idiots not to have thought of it earlier. As I was saying, Mr. Baldwin here shouldn't sail the boat because of his . . . err . . ."

"Criminal record?" the other supplied.

"Well, yes. That would put you too much in jeopardy. And Lord Montague can't sail the boat because he's always being followed. So the obvious solution is for them to trade places. Mr. Baldwin here will have to be Lord Montague for a bit."

"That's an obvious solution?" Jane remarked dryly. "And just how is that to be accomplished? They're hardly look-alikes."

"Now just listen a moment. It's simple really. Lord Montague will 'sneak' to the stables, with Newbright close behind, of course. He'll take out his famous curricle— which is, of course, umistakable. And by all means he must wear that jaunty curly-brimmed beaver of his. And his five-caped greatcoat. He'll set off down the road at a fairly rapid clip. That's crucial. Oh, by the by, Mr. Baldwin, you *do* drive?"

"I'm a nonesuch."

"Good. For it will be important to keep well ahead of Mr. Newbright, but still not lose him.

"But as I was saying, Lord Montague will drive to a designated spot where you'll be hiding. You'll rapidly change places . . . and coats and hats. And you'll fly down the Dover Road so fast that Mr. Newbright will never know the difference." She beamed at her companions expecting accolades. None were forthcoming.

"In the meantime," she added with just the slightest edge of pique to her tone, "you do understand, don't you, that Lord Montague and Mr. West will be on their way to France. I happen to think it's a famous plan."

"There are a few flaws in it." Jane sounded waspish. "For instance, what does Edward here say when Mr. Newbright finally overtakes him?"

"The object is for him not to be overtaken."

"If he isn't, then it will appear that Lord Montague had indeed smuggled Mr. West away to France. The only variation from the real truth will be that Mr. Newbright will believe they sailed from Dover and not from here."

"Oh."

"Exactly."

"Well, then, Mr. Newbright will have to overtake Mr. Baldwin—though not for ages, of course—and be made to look the fool."

"And when this happens, just how is Edward expected to explain the fact he's driving his lordship's rig and wearing his coat and hat? He will, of course, be an accessory to a crime."

"Oh."

"Exactly."

"Well," said Jemima, refusing to be daunted, "we'll just have to come up with a good explanation for his behavior, that's all."

"That should be simple enough," Jane said witheringly. "There should be all sorts of acceptable reasons for Edward here to have borrowed Montague's rig—and his coat and hat— and to be racing down the Dover Road in the dead of night."

"If it's any help," Mr. Baldwin offered with a perfectly straight face, "I do happen to own a curly-brimmed beaver. Not quite as elegant as his lordship's, alas, but its silhouette by night should pass muster. Unfortunately my greatcoat can only boast three capes, but in the dark and at a distance, Newbright won't likely count 'em. That leaves only the rig to be explained."

Jemima was thinking furiously. "Eureka!" She slapped her forehead again, to its detriment. "It's the very thing. I should have thought of it right off, but it's difficult to be creative under the circumstances." She gave Jane a speaking look. "An elopement! After all," she smiled apologetically, "that is the sort of thing one might expect of you, Mr. Baldwin."

"All by myself?"

"No, of course not. I'll come with you. That is to say, I'll be waiting with you when Lord Montague drives up. Let's see now. I'll need to wear a greatcoat or something so that I could be mistaken for a man. Why, this is perfect. For it did not make a great deal of sense for you to be driving to Dover alone. I had hoped that Mr. Newbright would conclude that Mr. West was hidden there. But this is much, much better. Famous, in fact."

"It really isn't, you know," Mr. Baldwin said gently. "We cannot allow you to ruin yourself. Your reputation would be in shreds. Mr. West would not wish that. And I'm certain Lord Montague would never be a party to such a shocking enterprise."

"But—" Jemima had begun when Jane cut her short.

"Do you know, Edward, I really think it would work. With one small alteration. You will elope with me. No one will find that at all wonderful. Or connect it with Mr. West. We shall simply 'borrow' the famous curricle. For reasons of speed, you understand, for I should not like to be overtaken a second time. Yes, I do think this is quite believable. So I'm game if you are."

"Oh, but I had not intended to involve you," Jemima protested. "It could be most unpleasant for you."

"Not in the least. I'm quite accustomed by now to being fodder for the gossipmongers. But you're young, marriageable. An elopement would sink you below reproach, Jemima."

"Besides," Baldwin pointed out practically, "you've got no fortune. No one would believe in *our* elopement."

There was a bit more wrangling back and forth, but at last it was decided and the details of the scheme worked out. Now all that was left was to make his lordship privy to the plan.

Chapter Twenty-one

JEMIMA AND JANE had been home for the better part of two hours before Lord Montague returned to the court. He came striding into the hall in a rush of cold air. "Oh, you can leave the door open," he said to Riggs who had jumped to close it. "I expect Mr. Newbright's right behind me." Jemima, who'd been lurking at the head of the stairs, now passed him nonchalantly as he came up them. "Meet me in the library as soon as you can," she whispered.

"For heaven's sake, was it necessary to dress?" she fumed when he finally joined her there. He'd changed his riding clothes for a russet-colored coat and white tightfitting pantaloons that showed off his muscular legs to a disturbing advantage. Jemima found herself wishing she'd not worn her dull brown round dress.

"I did rather smell of the stables," he replied a bit defensively. "Besides, we're trying to appear normal, are we not?" To illustrate his point he went over to pull a book at random from the shelf before seating himself across the table from her.

"*Practical Piety*," she read the title aloud. "Do you call that normal?"

"Get on with it before someone comes in here. Did you find Jonathan?"

"I know where he is. In general terms. And how he's to be rescued." She paused smugly, then went on to fill him in on what had been decided.

When she'd finished, he was looking at her with new respect. "You know, that's really brilliant. Was it your idea?"

"Mostly." Her attempt at modesty was a distinct failure.

"Of course, there is one thing," he mused. "I'll be missed. Still, it doesn't really matter what anyone suspects as long as nothing can be proved."

"We've thought of a plan to cover the night of the elopement. It involves your getting sick again right away, I'm afraid. Do you think you can manage a relapse?"

"No more rouge spots, please." He recoiled in mock horror. "Besides, no one would believe it."

"Well, they might, considering the weird course your measles seem to take," she chuckled. "But a second round of them wasn't what I had in mind. You simply got up too soon from your sick bed, so now you've come down with the grippe or something. What we'll do is put Bess, my maid, in your bed with a night cap. So unless someone comes up and actually peers at her face they'll think it's you."

"Good God!"

Lord Montague digested this in silence for a bit and then said softly, his enigmatic eyes intent upon her face, "There's one thing I still don't understand, Jemima. Just why are you doing all this?"

"I'm not doing anything at all, actually," she said regretfully. "My original idea was to elope with Mr.

Baldwin myself, but they insisted that it would not be the thing."

"I should think not."

"Well, it probably wouldn't be convincing anyhow. Though I don't see why I couldn't get to Dover, then pretend to change my mind. That's what Jane plans to do. But she doesn't feel that I could get away with it the way that she can."

"You haven't answered my question, you know."

"Why am I involved? Well, mostly because of my sister. She idolizes Mr. West, you see. By the by," she broke off, "what is he like? Is he, err, ah, married?"

"Good lord, no," he chuckled. "To tell the truth, I think Jonathan is a bit scared of women. He's only a firebrand with his quill in hand, after the Regent's done something particularly outrageous."

"Well, no one could possibly be frightened of Clarissa. Not that they're ever likely to meet," she sighed.

"You never know. If we can save his hide, well, France isn't a million miles away. Perhaps in a year or so Georgie-Porgie can be prevailed upon to forgive him. The Regent's not really such a bad sort, you know.

"But," he switched the subject back once more, "you said you became involved in this coil *mostly* because of your sister." His eyes grew more intense. "What's your other reason?"

She looked embarrassed. "I really don't wish to say."

"Oh, come, Jemima," he coaxed softly. "Surely after all this, you don't have to stand on points with me."

"Well then—if you really want the truth—you see

I didn't wish to come here at all. As you know, they'd asked Clarissa. And though Mama seemed to think it was all right to send me in her place, I knew it would put my aunt and Marcus in a pucker. We've never got on, you see."

"I noticed." His face was solemn, but his eyes betrayed him.

"But Mama insisted. It was an opportunity, she said, to broaden my horizons."

"Meet some eligible suitor you mean?"

"Yes," she sighed. "Mr. Newbright, as it turned out."

"How ghastly for you."

"Well, it was rather. But then as things worked out, that part didn't really matter."

"Why not?" he breathed.

"Because," her face grew animated, "it has all been the most incredible adventure. You can't begin to imagine, given the life you lead, how deadly dull it is at home. Nothing ever happens. Absolutely nothing. But on this one trip I've been in a coach wreck—oh, I'll admit, that made me furious at the time—but if it hadn't happened I wouldn't have met up with Mr. Baldwin, who was a mystery in himself. Then there was the excitement of realizing that you'd been shot—"

"I'm glad *you* found it exhilarating."

"Oh, I didn't mean it like that. No need to take offense. I'm simply trying to explain that a visit I thought would be tedious to the extreme has turned into a glorious adventure. So that's really why I became involved. For the sheer excitement of it. Surely you can understand that."

"I'm beginning to," he answered dryly.

It was her turn to look intently at him now. "Oh, for heaven's sake. You thought I'd done it all for you, didn't you? Come on, admit it."

"Well, would that be so wonderful?"

"Evidently not. Ever since I got here everyone else has been expecting me to make some kind of cake of myself over you, so I can't imagine why I thought you, of all people, would be an exception."

"Just what do you mean," he bristled, "by me, of all people?"

"Well you're accustomed to having females fall at your feet by the droves, now aren't you?"

"Certainly. I simply step over them or kick them aside. Whichever."

"No need to take offense. It's an enviable state of affairs, I imagine. At least it is if one is rich as Croesus and of a rakish disposition."

"Which I am, of course."

"Well, aren't you? That's what everyone says about you. By the by," she blurted before she thought, "do you have a particular mistress that you give a carte blanche to, or do you play the field?"

"You really haven't any notion of propriety at all, have you?" he glared.

"Well, you yourself said that there was no reason for us to stand on points. But I do beg pardon if I've been offensive."

"You have been. But to answer your question, at least in part, I've never established any love nests. I'm not that big a fool."

"No, I expect you're totally up to snuff. That's why I thought it absurd for everyone to keep warning me that you might try and give me a slip on the shoulder. Why, you must be used to the crème de la crème."

"If you're fishing for compliments, Miss Forbes, I refuse to rise to bait."

She colored. "It did rather sound like that, didn't it? But believe me, I never would have done so intentionally."

"Oh, what the devil. Just because you've walked all over my own self-esteem, there's no need to tear down yours. Believe me, when it comes to looks, Miss Forbes, you *are* the crème de la crème. Disposition is, of course, quite another matter. You are without a doubt the most irritating, contrary, impossible female— Still," he broke off suddenly to muse aloud, "I can't help but wonder how it would have been if we'd met under more normal circumstances."

"Oh, I'm sure that if you'd made me one of your flirts I'd have swooned at your feet like all the rest. There's no need to be in the least concerned about your appeal."

"Do you know," he said pleasantly, "I'm amazed that someone hasn't throttled you years ago."

"I can assure you that I'm not usually thought of—" she began heatedly, then pulled herself in check. "Well, we've certainly wandered from the subject, haven't we? To get back to the matter in hand, are you quite sure now you know just what to do?"

"Yes, General." He saluted briskly. "The moment I leave here, I'll go into a rapid decline and take to my bed. I'll get up bravely for dinner, still not feeling quite the thing. After cigars and brandy, I shall declare that I need a breath of fresh air first, but then I mean to return to bed. God forbid that it should rain! I'll go to the stables, get my rig and drive like the devil's behind me up the carriage drive. At this point Newbright, who has followed me, of course, should be commandeering a rig to give chase. Baldwin, with Miss Lawford, will be lurking behind the gate pillars to take my place. I'll jump out. They'll leap in. Baldwin will drive slowly enough at first for Newbright to hove into sight, at which point our secretary will see two persons in my rig. 'Ah ha!', he'll exclaim aloud, 'Montague and West!' He'll then give chase. Baldwin, with my superior equipage, will easily outrun him to Dover.

"In the meantime I hare off to the beach on foot—that's the flaw in your plan as far as I'm concerned—where Jonathan will be hidden in Baldwin's boat, under canvas or something, and we'll push off for France. I'll settle him in there and be back with the tide."

"You certainly make it sound simple." Jemima was looking a bit off-color suddenly. "But what if something should go wrong? I'll never forgive myself if you're caught."

"Second thoughts, General?"

"Well," she swallowed, "I must admit that up to this point it more or less seemed like some sort of game. Now I realize it's in dead earnest. Are you sure you're up to it? The arm, I mean."

"Except for being a bit sore to the touch, it's fine. But thanks for asking. And don't fret so. It's a good plan. And I'm an excellent sailor. Your part is over. You can just relax and enjoy Christmas Eve."

"That sounds unlikely," she answered. "But we'd best go now before someone catches us in this tête-à-tête." She rose and carried her book back to the shelf. "Don't you want to take something to read with you besides *Practical Piety*? You're going to be in that bed for quite some time, you know."

"Perhaps you're right." He came to stand behind her and peer over her shoulder.

"Have you read *Roderick Random*?" she asked as her eyes lit on a favorite novel and she pulled it from the shelf. "It should take your mind off—"

The book fell from her fingers as she was spun round, then clasped tightly against the superfine coat. "Just what do you think you're—" she'd begun when his lips put a stop to all utterance.

This time there were no distractions. Jemima regretted her surrender to the bone-melting sensation stealing over her, but for her life's worth she could think of no good reason to resist. Cooperation, in fact, appeared the order of the day. Her arms seemed to find their way around his neck of their own accord, while she rose on tiptoe in order to participate more fully in the action.

When Montague had reluctantly broken off the lingering embrace, Jemima leaned against his chest a moment longer to regain her equilibrium. After a deep breath or two, she managed to look up. "What brought that on?" she whispered hoarsely.

"Mistletoe, what else?" He grinned wickedly down at her. "Merry Christmas."

"I should have known," she muttered as he planted a chaste kiss on her forehead for good measure and then left her standing there. She stared dazedly at the closed library door for the longest time and then looked upward.

"Blast his eyes!"

There was no mistletoe anywhere in sight.

Chapter Twenty-two

IT SHOULD HAVE been, under normal circumstances, a marvelous Christmas Eve. Certainly Sir Walter had done everything in his power to achieve it. The company, gathered in the great hall before dinner, gasped at the size of the Yule log that crackled in the enormous fireplace. It had required four men to carry it in; the grate had been removed to accommodate it. And in the dining chamber, the tall Christmas candles on the sideboard seemed to blaze forth far more cheer than all the ordinary candles put together. Minced pies held pride of place between them, a fact which ordinarily would have set Jemima's mouth awater from the moment she took her place at the groaning board. But in her present state of agitation, her mouth was dry as dust.

She kept telling herself not to stare toward the head of the table. But her self paid no attention. She risked a peek and saw the handkerchief Lord Montague had held in his hand for the entire evening leap once more toward his nose. His sneeze reverberated throughout the room.

Don't overdo it, she thought as the people nearest him appeared to inch away.

His lordship could have had a fine career on the stage, she'd earlier decided, had he not been to the manor born. From the moment he'd tottered down the stairs into the hall it had been more obvious that he was in the throes of severe grippe. Too obvious, in fact. Mr. Newbright, seated next to Jemima, was regarding his lordship suspiciously.

A harper had been installed in the corner of the dining chamber. Most of his strumming had been drowned out by the boisterous conversation and laughter. But at the conclusion of the feast, Sir Walter tapped a knife upon his crystal goblet and invited his guests's attention for the young villager's final song. "An ancient ditty, familiar to our ancestors," Sir Walter called it, and nodded toward the musician who began to sing.

Now Christmas is come,
Let us beat up the drum,
And call our neighbors together;
And when they appear,
Let us make them such cheer,
As will keep out the wind and the weather.

After a few more stanzas and a round of applause, more enthusiastic than Jemima felt the young tenor's efforts called for, the dinner broke up and the ladies took their temporary leave.

Back in the great hall, they gathered round the fire, which one young matron declared was bound to go on burning until the following Christmas. "Where is Miss Jane?" one of the relatives inquired.

"She's gone to attend a tenant's lying in." Lady Lawford sniffed her disapproval. "I think it entirely unsuitable at any time. And Christmas Eve! Well, I don't mind saying that I spoke my mind frankly on the subject. But I couldn't prevent her going. Sir

Walter encourages her, you know. It fits right in with this old fiefdom—or whatever—notion of his."

"Well, I only hope *she* doesn't wind up with the grippe," someone else observed. "Did you notice how often his lordship sneezed tonight?"

There followed an animated discussion of Lord Montague's delicacy (a result, it was decided, of his noble blood) that Jemima found enormously diverting. It was interrupted by the entrance of the gentlemen, sans not only Lord Montague but Mr. Newbright. So far, the plan was moving along on schedule.

The evening proved interminable. There was dancing at first, and Jemima gladly joined in the set in hopes that the rollicking country dances would keep her mind off the drama that was being acted out, in the Greek manner, somewhere off stage. It didn't.

And after that, her cousin Marcus decided to play troubadour. He lounged against the mantlepiece in a studied manner while plucking his guitar and directing a French love song soulfully at Miss Evans. Since her cousin's voice was as off-key as his French pronunciation, Jemima was much relieved when his father waved him to a halt. The relief was short-lived, however. Sir Walter obviously had no ear. His only objection, it appeared, was to Marcus's choice of song. Once the troubadour had switched to old English carols, Sir Walter sat back and tapped his foot with parental pride.

Though long delayed by the revelry taking place in the servants' hall, the tea board did at last appear. And the company did at last bid one another a good night and a Merry Christmas, with Sir Walter chuckling that there was no better night in the year for sleeping, since, as the Bard himself had written, "No spirit dare stir abroad . . . so hallow'd and so gracious is the time."

That's what he thinks, Jemima thought as she picked up her candle in the hall to light her way to bed. The spirits were stirring abroad all right. She just wished she knew how they were faring. Were Montague and Mr. West far out in the Channel? And when would Jane be back? Did Mr. Newbright catch up with them after all? She did hope not. Though Jane claimed not to mind the scandal, it assuredly would not be pleasant for her.

With all these thoughts churning around in her head, Jemima was convinced that she'd never get to sleep. But the last thing she remembered was the sound of music coming from outside, which she concluded must be carolers come to serenade them from the neighboring village. The next thing she knew, someone was shaking her roughly awake.

"Oh, miss, do get up. Hurry!"

The young chambermaid had obviously dressed in a tearing rush. Her cap was askew, her buttons done wrong and her apron untied. "Such a to-do you can't possibly imagine. And Lady Lawford wants to see you right away."

As Jemima entered her bedchamber, Lady Lawford's voice cracked with anger. "You're responsible for this, I know you are!" She waved a letter back and forth under her niece's nose. Her dishabille far outdid Jemima's who had at least taken time to brush her hair and fasten her dressing gown in a proper manner. "It's all your fault!" her ladyship shrieked.

"Now, now, now, m'dear, you mustn't be so hasty." Sir Walter, fully clad in sober clothing, shook his head gently at his wife. "I'm sure Jemima knows as little of this affair as we do."

"Don't you believe it!" It was obvious that Marcus, too, had been roused from sleep. His nightshirt, cap, dressing gown, and slippers did little for his dignity but did not reduce one iota the ferocity of his glare. "Why she and Aunt Jane became bosom bows in no time at all. Which was deuced odd if you ask my opinion. And if you believe they were merely carrying food to the tenants all those times, well then you're queer in the attic, sir. Besides, she and Baldwin appeared thick as thieves. Ha!" He snorted at his accidental witticism. "Thick as thieves! That's good, that is. Why, I'll bet you a monkey it was her idea to go to his place for mistletoe. Monty would never have done such a thing of his own accord."

"Would someone mind telling me what this is all about?" Jemima inquired with what she considered remarkable forbearance.

"As if you didn't know," Marcus began but was frowned into silence by his father.

"It seems my sister has eloped with Mr. Baldwin."

Jemima's mouth fell open. "She has? Truly? Oh, but I don't think—" She quickly closed her mouth again.

"And the worst of it is," Marcus's voice shook with indignation, "that they helped themselves to Monty's rig to do it in."

"That is hardly the worst of it." Lady Lawford glared at her only child for possibly the first time in his life. "The worst of it is that your aunt is dragging our name through the mud once more by actually marrying that . . . that . . . gaol bird."

"But are you sure there's no mistake?" Jemima asked.

"You know damned well there's not," Marcus retorted. "I'm still convinced you put her up to it."

"That will do, Marcus." His father silenced him with a frown and then turned to Jemima. "There's no mistake. An ostler arrived from Dover a bit ago, returning Lord Montague's rig and delivering a note from Jane saying that she and Baldwin were taking a packet to France where they'll be married. Marcus thought that perhaps you were privy to their plans. Were you, Jemima?"

"Why, no, I'd no idea they were actually eloping," she was able to reply with perfect truth. "But I will say though, I think it's famous."

"Famous! *Famous*!"

Jemima regarded her aunt with alarm. She appeared on the verge of an hysterical fit. Her massive body quivered. "My sister-in-law runs off—for the second time, mind you—with a fortune-hunting criminal, and my own flesh and blood calls it famous!"

"Well, I don't happen to think he is a fortune hunter." Jemima courageously stuck to her guns. "Mr. Baldwin does have a competency now, you know. And I'm not sure that being incarcerated for debt makes one a criminal in the truest sense. But the main thing is, I'm convinced he really loves her."

"Ingrate!" Lady Lawford shrieked. "And after all I've tried to do for you. To think that I've nursed a viper in my bosom. I want you out of my house immediately. Immediately! Do you hear me?"

"Yes, ma'am."

"Now, now, m'dear, be reasonable," Sir Walter intervened. "This is Christmas Day. She can't possibly leave now."

"He's right, you know," Marcus chimed in regretfully. "Coaches won't be running."

"The first thing in the morning, then," her ladyship compromised. "And don't let me see you in the meantime. And I intend to write your mother immediately. You may be quite sure of that, miss. I shall tell her that I now wash my hands of her entire family. For if this is the thanks I get after trying to find a husband for one of her five daughters, well the other four need not expect any help from me."

Chapter Twenty-three

JEMIMA SPENT ALL Christmas Day, from church in the morning to a sumptuous Christmas dinner complete with boar's head, waiting on tenterhooks for Lord Montague's return. When it never happened, she reluctantly climbed in bed to at last fall asleep only to dream of his little craft being capsized and sunk in the treacherous channel.

Then on the following morning she bade a tearful good-bye to Bess, whom she left behind to fully recover, and followed a footman down the long carriage drive to the gate. After he had flagged down the coach from Dover and she had climbed to the top to shiver in the misty cold, Jemima realized that the very worst part of her Christmas visit was that she'd never, ever know what had transpired.

Well, of course she'd know it if Lord Montague actually drowned. For if calamity of any kind struck such a prominent personage, the London papers would be full of it. Besides, daylight had greatly reduced the sort of fear that had terrorized her throughout the night. Lord Montague had, most likely, simply decided to stay awhile and sample the French delights with no thought for the fact that she was worried sick, besides perishing to know just how her scheme had worked. Oh well. Perhaps he'd get in touch with the Baldwins one of these days. Jemima then smiled to herself as the coach picked up speed and she tightened the strings of her bonnet. Squire and Mrs. Baldwin. That had quite a nice ring to it, she thought.

She also took comfort in the fact that her uncle, at any rate, had not been horrified by Jane's elopement. After she'd been banished from Lady Lawford's presence, he had taken her aside and confided that he, too, thought his sister might find happiness as mistress of Baldwin Hall. Also he'd suggested kindly that she not take her aunt's "humors" too seriously. "Ada's quite excitable, you know. But she soon gets over these little crochets. And of course we'll not neglect our duty to your mother and your sisters. Family is everything. You'll realize that, Jemima, as you grow older."

That had certainly come as a relief. Knowing she could have sunk all her sisters' hopes was lowering indeed. Well hadn't she warned her mother that it would be a grave mistake for her to visit Lawford Court?

Even so, Jemima had never dreamed of the devastating consequences to her own well-being. While she might not approve of Lord Montague and all he stood for, she was painfully aware that she was doomed to recall his kisses till the day she died. Which was totally unfair, since he'd no doubt forgotten them already. But the word fair didn't apply to the Lord Montagues of this world.

Enough of this! She was not going to turn into one of those languishing females wasting away for love in the pages of the horrid mysteries she sometimes read. She forced herself to try to find some beauty in the winter-blighted scenery they were passing through and even went so far as to exchange a few pleasantries with the elderly man shivering under layers of shawls beside her. She was glad then for the distraction of rapidly approaching hoof beats and turned her head to look.

"Oh, my word!" She clutched at one of her neighbor's shawls.

A pair of perfectly matched grays pulling a flashy curricle—yes, it was black and red—was bearing down upon them. Its driver, wearing a jaunty beaver and a five-caped greatcoat, was on his feet. His long black whip snaked its way out over the horses' heads, to crack like a pistol shot above their ears.

"The bloody fool's trying to pass on this narrow stretch!" the coachman yelled. "Hang on!" The coach rocked precariously as the cursing driver jerked his four horses from the center of the road amid a volley of shouts and screams from the panicked passengers.

As the coach at last began to steady itself, the dapper young driver of the racing curricle commanded the coachman to pull up.

"You . . . you . . . numbskull! Ninnyhammer!" Jemima shouted over the roar of the other passengers as the coachman, swearing a blue streak, complied.

"Well, I had to catch you, didn't I?" Lord Montague grinned as he vaulted from his rig, ignoring the pandemonium he had created, and held up his arms. "Come on. Jump down. I'm driving you home."

"Didn't one coach wreck satisfy your blood lust?" she asked once he'd situated her in the passenger's seat and they were tooling down the highway, leaving the public coach far behind.

"That's gratitude for you. When I got back from my trip abroad and heard that you'd been banished,

I was sure you'd be dying to know how your rescue scheme worked out, so I hurried along to tell you. But I should have known that my efforts would just bring on another tongue-banging about my driving skill, which is damn good in case you aren't noticing." He glanced back over his shoulder and, appearing satisfied with the distance now between them and the coach, slowed down this team to rest them.

"I'm sorry." Jemima managed to apologize with a modicum of grace despite the letdown she was feeling over the reason he had chased her down. "Tell me all about it."

He proceeded to do so, with a great deal more detail about the art of navigation than she really cared to hear. Then he finished up with a lengthy description of the rooms he'd found for Jonathan. "He'll stay in Calais for a while till he decides what's best to be done. So 'all's well that ends well,' as prosy old Shakespeare said."

"Well, that is a relief." Jemima tried, a bit unsuccessfully, to pack enthusiasm into her voice. "And I really do appreciate the trouble you've taken to tell me of it."

"Oh, well," he cut his eyes her way, "that's not the only reason I chased you down, you know."

"It isn't?"

"No, indeed." There was a long, pregnant pause. "I promised Jonathan, you see, that I'd deliver a letter for him to your sister. And I needed someone to show me the way."

"Oh, you did, did you?" she bristled. "Well, you could have waited a bit and taken Bess, you know. It would have saved her the coach trip."

"Damn, so I could have," he grinned. "Now why

didn't I think of that? I collect I must simply have wanted your company, Jemima. Now there's a lowering thought. It must have been that last kiss that did it," he mused aloud. "Of course I kept telling myself all the way across the Channel and back that I really shouldn't exaggerate its effect. After all, I was in a weakened condition—having first been shot, then taken with the measles *and* the grippe. No wonder I found your kiss so devastating. By the by, how was it for you?"

"It was . . . nice."

"Nice? *Nice*!" he glared. "You have the gall to call an experience that rocked me right down to the soles of my Hessians 'nice'?"

"Well, how should I know?" she retorted. "I haven't your experience in such matters."

"Well, then take it from me, you pathetic green 'un, it was a regular Waterloo of a kiss."

"Oh."

"And that, as if you haven't known it all along, is why I've chased you down to take you home. After all, I have to know where you live, don't I, if I'm to," his five capes shuddered, "come there a-courting."

"Is that what you wish to do?" she managed to ask.

"It's what I have to do," he answered glumly. "That is," he brightened, "unless you'd prefer to just tool on to Gretna Green this very minute?"

"You know I can't elope."

"I was afraid that was what you'd say."

They rode in silence for a bit while she tried to digest his words and quite failed to do so. The looks she stole upward at him from beneath her lowered lashes betrayed her inward struggle.

His eyes danced with mischief at her obvious confusion. "By the by, Miss Forbes, you do realize, do you not, that I'm a splendid catch. Far above your touch, if I may say so."

"Above my touch!" She snapped out of her reverie to glare at him. And then her eyes narrowed as she carefully measured the distance from his lips to hers. "Above my touch? Oh I think not, Lord Montague."

Miss Jemima Forbes raised herself up off the red leather seat, clasped her arms around the five-caped greatcoat, and incontrovertibly proved her point.